SO YESTERDAY

SO YESTERDAY

A NOVEL BY

SCOTT WESTERFELD

razOr
bill
NEW YORK

So Yesterday

RAZORBILL
Published by the Penguin Group
Penguin Young Readers Group
345 Hudson Street, New York, New York 10014, U.S.A.
Penguin Group (USA) Inc., 375 Hudson Street, New York, New York 10014, U.S.A
Penguin Books Canada Ltd, 10 Alcorn Avenue, Toronto, Ontario, Canada M4V 3B2
(a division of Pearson Penguin Canada, Inc.)
Penguin Books Ltd, 80 Strand, London WC2R 0RL, England
Penguin Ireland, 25 St Stephen's Green, Dublin 2, Ireland (a division of Penguin Books Ltd)
Penguin Group (Australia), 250 Camberwell Road, Camberwell, Victoria 3124, Australia
(a division of Pearson Australia Group Pty Ltd)
Penguin Books India Pvt Ltd, 11 Community Centre, Panchsheel Park,
New Delhi – 110 017, India
Penguin Group (NZ), Cnr Airborne and Rosedale Roads, Albany, Auckland, New Zealand
(a division of Pearson New Zealand Ltd)
Penguin Books (South Africa) (Pty) Ltd, 24 Sturdee Avenue, Rosebank,
Johannesburg 2196, South Africa

Penguin Books Ltd, Registered Offices: 80 Strand, London WC2R 0RL, England

10 9 8 7 6 5 4 3 2 1

Text design by Christopher Grassi

Library of Congress Cataloging-in-Publication Data

Westerfeld, Scott.
  So yesterday / by Scott Westerfeld.— 1st ed.
    p. cm.
  Summary: Hunter Braque, a New York City teenager who is paid by corporations to spot what is
"cool," combines his analytical skills with girlfriend Jen's creative talents to find a missing person
and thwart a conspiracy directed at the heart of consumer culture.
  ISBN 1-59514-000-X (hardcover)
  [1. Missing persons—Fiction. 2. New York (N.Y.)—Fiction. 3. Adventure and
adventurers—Fiction. 4. Mystery and detective stories.] I. Title.
  PZ7.W5197So 2004
  [Fic]—dc22
  2004002302

Printed in the United States of America

To the Innovators.
You know who you are.

SO YESTERDAY

CHAPTER ZERO

WE ARE ALL AROUND YOU.

You don't think about us much because we are invisible. Well, not exactly invisible. A lot of us have hair dyed in four colors, or wear five-inch platform sneakers, or carry enough metal in our skin that it's a hassle getting on an airplane. Quite visible, actually, come to think of it.

But we don't wear signs saying what we are. After all, if you knew what we were up to, we couldn't work our magic. We have to observe carefully and push and prompt you in ways you don't notice. Like good teachers, we let you think you've discovered the truth on your own.

And you need us. Someone has to guide you, to mold you, to make sure that today turns into yesterday on schedule. Because frankly, without us to monitor the situation, who knows what would get crammed down your throats?

It's not like you can just start making your own decisions, after all.

So, if we're supposed to be secret, why am I writing this?

Well, that's a long story. That's *this* story, the one you're holding in your hands.

It's about how I met Jen. She isn't one of us or one of you, either. She's on top of the whole pyramid, quietly making her contribution. Trust me, you need her. We all do.

It's also about the Jammers, who I'm pretty sure really do exist. Probably. *If* they're real, then they're crazy smart, and they've got big plans. They're the bad guys, the ones trying to bring the system down. They want to make people like me redundant, unnecessary, ridiculous.

They want to set you free.

And the funny thing is, I *think* I'm on their side.

Okay. Is that enough previews for you? Can you pay attention long enough for me to do this in order? Is it time for the feature presentation?

Let's get started, then.

ONE

"CAN I TAKE A PICTURE OF YOUR SHOE?"

"Huh?"

"Shoelaces, actually. The way you tied them."

"Oh. Yeah, sure, I guess. Pretty skate, huh?"

I nodded. That week *skate* meant "cool," like *dope* or *rad* once did. And this girl's laces *were* cool. Fuzzy and red, they looped through the middle eyelet repeatedly on one side, spreading out in a fan on the other. Kind of like the old rising-sun Japanese flag, but sideways.

She was about seventeen, the same as me. Gray sweatshirt over camo pants, hair dyed so black that it turned blue when the sun hit it through the trees. The shoes were off-brand black runners, the logo markings erased with a black laundry pen.

Definitely an Innovator, I thought. They tend to specialize, looking like Logo Exiles until you get close, until you see that one flourish. All their energies focused on a single element.

Like shoelaces.

I pulled out my phone and pointed it at her foot.

Her eyes widened and she gave the Nod. My phone for that month, made by a certain company in Finland, was getting a lot of the Nod, the slight incline of the head that means, *I saw that in a magazine and I already want it.* Of course, at another level the Nod also means, *Now that I've seen an actual person with that phone, I really, really have to get one.*

At least, that's what the certain Finnish company was hoping when they mailed it to me. So there I was, doing two jobs at once.

The phone took its picture, signaling success by playing a sample of a certain dysfunctional father saying, "Sweet, sweet chocolate." The sample did not get the Nod, and I made a mental note to change it. Homer was out; Lisa was in.

I looked at the image on the phone's little screen, which looked clear enough to copy the lacework back at home.

"Thanks."

"No problem." An edge of suspicion in her voice now. Exactly why was I taking a picture of her laces?

There was a moment of awkward silence, the kind that sometimes follows after taking a picture of a stranger's shoe. You think by now I'd be used to it.

I turned away to look at the river. I'd run into my shoelace Innovator in the East River Park, a strip of grass and promenade between the FDR Drive and the water. It's one of the few places where you can tell that Manhattan is an island.

She was carrying a basketball, probably had been shooting hoops on the weedy courts under Manhattan Bridge.

I was here working, like I said.

A big container ship eased by on the water, as slow as a minute hand. Across the river was Brooklyn, looking industrial, the Domino Sugar factory waiting patiently to be turned into an art gallery or housing for millionaires.

I was about to smile once more and keep on walking, but she spoke up.

"What else does it do?"

"My phone?" The list of features was on my tongue, but this was the part of the job I didn't like (which is why you will read *no* product placement in these pages, if I can possibly help it). I shrugged, trying not to sound like a salesman. "MP3 player, date book, texting. And the camera can shoot like ten seconds of video."

She bit her lip, gave another Nod.

"Very crappy video," I admitted. It was not my job to lie.

"Can you call people on it?"

"Sure, it—" Then I realized she had to be kidding. "Yes, you can actually call people on it."

Her smile was even better than her shoelaces.

When Alexander Graham Bell invented the telephone, he imagined everybody in the country having one big party line. We'd all listen to concerts on the phone, or maybe everyone would pick up and sing the national anthem together. Of course, a somewhat more popular use of the telephone turned out to be one person talking to one other person.

The first computers were designed for naval gunnery and code breaking. And when the Internet was created, it was supposed to be for controlling the country after a nuclear war. But guess what? Most people use them for e-mailing and IM-ing. One person communicating with one other person.

See the pattern?

"My name's Hunter," I said, returning her smile.

"Jen."

I nodded. "Jennifer was the most popular girl's name in the 1970s and number two in the 1980s."

"Huh?"

"Oh, sorry." Sometimes the facts in my head get bored and decide to take a walk in my mouth. Frequently this is a bad thing.

She shook her head. "No, I know what you mean. There's Jens all over the place these days. I was thinking of changing it."

"Jennifer did drop to fourteenth place in the 1990s. Possibly from overexposure." I winced when I realized I'd said this out loud. "But I think it's a nice name."

Great save, huh?

"Me too, but I get bored, you know? Same name all the time."

"Rebranding," I said, nodding. "Everyone's doing it."

She laughed, and I found that we'd started walking together. On a Thursday the park was pretty empty, mostly joggers, dog walkers, and a couple of old guys trying to catch something in the river. We ducked under their fishing lines, which flickered from invisible to brilliant in the summer sun. Behind the metal guardrail the river sloshed against concrete, agitated by a small boat motoring past.

"So, how's Hunter doing?" she asked. "The name, I mean."

"You really want to know?" I checked her smile for signs of derision. Not everyone appreciates the pleasures of socialsecurity.gov's name-ranking database.

"Absolutely."

"Well, it's no Jennifer, but it's moving up. Hunter was barely in the top four hundred when I was born, but it's a solid number thirty-two these days."

"Wow. So you were way ahead of the crowd."

"Yeah, I guess." I took a sidelong glance at her, wondering if she'd figured me out already.

Jen bounced the basketball once and let it rise into the air in front of her, ringing like a bell, before catching it with long fingers. She studied its longitude lines for a moment, spinning it before her green eyes like a globe.

"Of course, you wouldn't want your name to get *too* popular, would you?"

"That would suck," I agreed. "Witness the Britney epidemic of the mid-1990s."

She shuddered, and my phone rang. The theme from *The Twilight Zone,* right on cue.

"See?" I said, holding it up for Jen. "It's doing its phone thing."

"Impressive."

The display read *shugrrl,* which meant work.

"Hi, Mandy."

"Hunter? Are you doing anything?"

"Uh, not really."

"Can you do a tasting? It's kind of an emergency."

"Right now?"

"Yes. The client wants to put an advertisement on the air over the weekend, but they're not sure about it."

Mandy Wilkins always called her employers "the client," even though she'd worked for them for two years. They were a certain athletic shoe company named after a certain Greek god. Maybe she didn't like using four-letter words.

"I'm trying to get together whoever I can," Mandy said. "The client needs to make a decision in a couple of hours."

"How much does it pay?"

"Officially, just a pair."

"I've got way too many pairs," I said. A trunk full of shoes, not counting the ones I'd given away.

"How about fifty bucks? Out of my own pocket. I need you, Hunter."

"Okay, Mandy, whatever." I looked at Jen, who was scrolling absently through numbers, politely not listening, maybe a little saddened by how old and decrepit her own phone was (at least six months). I made a decision.

"Can I bring someone?"

"Uh, sure. We need more bodies. But are they . . . you know?"

Jen glanced at me, her eyes narrowing, beginning to realize that I was talking about her. The sun was catching more blue in her hair. I could see that she'd dyed a few slender strands bright purple, hidden underneath the black outer layers, letting glimpses of color through when the wind stirred her hair.

"Yeah. Definitely."

"A *what* tasting?"

"A cool tasting," I repeated. "But that's just what Mandy and I call them. Officially it's a 'focus group.'"

"Focusing on what?"

I told her the name of the client, which did *not* get the Nod.

"I know," I said. "But you get a free pair and fifty bucks." Once the words had left my mouth, I wondered if Mandy would cough up money for Jen as well as me. Well, if she didn't, Jen could always have my fifty. It was random money anyway.

But I wondered why I had invited her. Usually people in my profession don't like competition. It's one of those jobs, like politician, where there's already too many and everyone who's never tried it thinks they could do it better.

"Sounds kind of weird," Jen said.

I shrugged. "It's just a job. You get paid for your opinion."

"We look at shoes?"

"We watch an ad. Thirty seconds of TV, fifty bucks."

She looked into the currents of the river, having a two-second debate inside her head. I knew what she was thinking. *Am I being exploited? Am I selling out? Am I pulling a scam? Is this a trick? Who do I think I'm fooling? Who cares what I think, anyway?*

I've thought all those things myself.

She shrugged. "Hey. Fifty bucks."

I let my breath out, just then realizing I'd been holding it. "My thoughts exactly."

TWO

I RECOGNIZED HALF THE FACES AT THE TASTING. ANTOINE AND Trez, who worked at Dr. Jay's in the Bronx. Hiro Wakata, a board under his arm and headphones around his neck big enough to wear while parking an airplane with orange flashlights. The Silicon Alley crew, led by Lexa Legault behind chunky black eyeglass frames and clutching an MP3 player (made by a certain computer company whose name is a fruit often used in making pies). Hillary Winston-hyphen-Smith, having slummed her way over from Fifth Avenue, and Tina Catalina, whose pink T-shirt bore a slogan in English clearly composed by someone who spoke only Japanese. All of them looked very central casting.

I always felt a little out of place at these things. Most kids my age give away their opinions for free, thrilled just to be asked, so they never make it into the paid-focus-group circuit. As a result, Jen and I were the youngest people in the room. We were also the only ones who weren't dressed to represent. She was in Logo Exile uniform, and I was in cool-hunting camouflage. My non-brand T-shirt was the color of dried chewing gum, my corduroys the gray of a rainy day, my Mets cap (*not* Yankees) was pointed exactly straight ahead. Like a spy trying to blend into the crowd or a guy painting his apartment on laundry day, I avoid dressing cool for a focus group, which I figure is like showing up drunk to a wine tasting.

Antoine bumped my fist with his usual, "My man, Hunter," as he checked out Jen, wincing at the basketball under her arm, obviously thinking she was trying *way* too hard. But when his eyes caught her sneakers, they filled with pleasure.

"Nice laces."

"I saw them first," I said firmly. I'd already phoned the picture to Mandy, but if Antoine got a good look at them, the pattern would be spreading across the Bronx like a nasty flu. Or maybe they'd fizzle; you never knew.

He spread his hands in surrender and kept his eyes above her ankles. Honor among thieves.

I asked myself again why I had brought Jen here. To impress her? She was more likely to be seriously unimpressed. To impress *them?*

Who cared what they thought? Besides a handful of multibillion-dollar corporations and five or six trendy magazines?

"New girlfriend, Hunter?" Hillary of the Hyphen was also checking out Jen but in a completely different way, her blue eyes glazing over at Jen's Logo Exile ensemble. Hillary's black dress, black bag, and black shoes all had first and last names, their initials wrought in tiny gold buckles, and, like her, came from Fifth Avenue. She saved me the trouble of a comeback. "Oh, that's right. There wasn't an old one."

"Not as old as you, I'm sure," Jen said, not missing a beat.

Antoine whistled and spun on one heel with a squeak, clearing the deck. I pulled Jen over toward the chairs at the far side of the conference room, inside Mandy's clueless force field, out of range of Hillary's hundred-dollar claws (per hand).

"Hi, Hunter. Thanks for coming." Mandy was in serious client-wear, red and white and swooshed all over. She was peering down at the conference room's control panel, perhaps intimidated by its spaceship complexity.

She pressed a button, and blackout curtains jumped into motion, closing across the sixtieth-floor view of Central Park. A tentative stab later, wooden panels slid apart on one wall, revealing a TV that probably cost more than a Van Gogh but was much flatter.

"This is Jen."

"Nice laces," Mandy said, not bothering to look down, giving me the Nod. I saw a printout of my Jen-shoe photograph tucked into her clipboard, headed for mass production.

I sat Jen down and whispered, "She approves of you."

"This is all very weird," she answered.

"Duh."

Hillary Hyphen, who had recently reached the big two-oh, managed to close her mouth just as the lights began to fade.

The ad was set in the standard client fantasy world. It was nighttime and raining, and everything was wet and slick and beautiful, blue highlights gleaming from every metal surface. Three client-wearing models were in motion, each leaving their glamorous job to the beat of some German DJ's last-week remix of a song older than Hillary. One of the models was riding a beautiful motorcycle, another was on a bicycle with about fifty gears, and the last one (the woman, I noticed, these things being important) was on foot, her swooshes splashing through puddles reflecting Don't Walk signs.

"Oh, I get it. *Run*," Jen whispered.

I chuckled. There are only about twelve words in the client's language, but at least everyone is fluent.

Guess what? The three models were all headed to the same cool bar, which looked like a cross between a velvet couch factory and an operating room. They all ordered gleaming non-brand beers, looking thrilled to see each other, energized by their glamorous journeys across the fantasy world.

"Moving is fun," I whispered.

"Fun is good," Jen agreed.

The ad came to a tear-jerking end, our heroes leaving their beers untouched, having decided to keep moving. I guess they were going for a ride/run together? Wouldn't that be a little awkward? Whatever.

The lights came up.

"So"—Mandy spread her hands—"what do we think about 'Don't Walk'?"

It's funny that ads have titles, like little movies. But only the people who shoot them—and people like me—ever find out what those titles are.

"I liked the motorcycle," Tina Catalina said. "Japanese street bikes are way back."

Mandy's eyes went to Hiro Wakata, Lord of All Things with Wheels, who gave her the Nod, and she checked off a box on her clipboard. I'd thought American was in, but apparently the motorcycle gurus had decided otherwise.

"Skate remix," Lexa Legault offered, and the rest of the cyber-geeks nodded. The German DJ had their vote.

"A'ight shoes," Trez said, just to fill a brief silence. He and Antoine would have approved them months ago. Shoes that didn't make it in the Bronx were shipped off to Siberia, or New Jersey, or somewhere like that.

And besides, this tasting wasn't really about the shoes. It was about how all the little elements of the fantasy world added up or didn't.

"Was that Plastique, where they wound up?" Hillary Hyphen said. "That club is so last April."

Mandy checked her clipboard. "No, it's someplace in London." That shut Hillary up. The client was very clever, shooting the street scenes in New York and the interiors on another continent. You never wanted too much reality leaking into fantasy world. Reality gets old so fast.

"So we liked it?" Mandy asked the group. "Nothing felt wrong to you guys?"

She looked around expectantly. Spotting cool was only half our job. The more important half was spotting *un*cool before it made trouble. Like a race-car driver, the client worried more about crashing and burning than winning every lap.

The room stayed silent, and Mandy started to lower her clipboard happily to the table.

Then Jen spoke up.

"I was kind of bugged by the missing-black-woman formation."

Mandy blinked. "The what?"

Jen shrugged uncomfortably, feeling the eyes on her.

"Yeah, I know what you mean," I said, even though I didn't.

Jen took a slow breath, collecting her thoughts. "You know, the guy on the motorcycle was black. The guy on the bike was white. The woman was white. That's the usual bunch, you know? Like everybody's accounted for? Except not really. I call that the missing-black-woman formation. It kind of happens a lot."

It was quiet for another moment. But gears were spinning. Tina Catalina let out a long sigh of recognition.

"Like the *Mod Squad!*" she said.

"Yeah," Hiro chimed in, "or the three main characters in . . ." He named a certain trilogy of movies about cyber-reality and frozen kung fu whose title ends in an *X,* counts as a brand, and therefore will not grace these pages.

The floodgates broke. More comic books, movies, and TV shows tumbled off everyone's lips, a dozen stuffed-full pop-cultural memory banks rifled for examples of missing-black-woman formations until Mandy looked ready to cry.

She smacked the clipboard down.

"Is this something I should have *known about?*" she said sharply, sweeping her eyes around the table.

An unhappy silence fell over the conference room. I felt like an evil genius's henchman when something goes wrong in a certain series of secret agent films—as if Mandy might push a button on the control panel and we would be ejected, chairs and all, out the roof and into some lake in Central Park.

But Antoine cleared his throat and saved us all from the piranhas. "Hey, I never heard of this missing whatever before."

"Me neither," said Trez.

Lexa Legault had been tapping at her wireless notebook and said, "I got nothing. Zero relevant hits on . . ." She named a certain Web search tool whose name means a very large number. (Oh, forget it. I'm not going to get very far telling this story if I can't say "Google.")

"It's not a big deal," Jen said. "It just popped into my head, you know?"

"Yeah, like who watches *The Mod Squad* anymore?" Hillary Hyphen said, ending her eye roll with an exquisite glare at Jen. Hillary looked happy, at least, to see us kids put in our place.

The flush in Mandy's cheeks began to fade. She hadn't let the client miss a trend, a vital new concept, a youthquake. This was just some random thought that hadn't existed before today's meeting.

But as things wrapped up and Mandy paid me (for both of us, it turned out), she gave me a cold look, and I realized that I was in trouble. Something had been invented here that was going to spread. By the very nature of the meeting, the MBWF had had its last day of Google anonymity. The client would have about a week to get this advertisement on and off the air before Jen's rampaging new turn of phrase made it look as dated as a seventies cop show.

Mandy's look was telling me that I had done something inexcusable.

I had brought an Innovator to a cool tasting, where only Trendsetters were allowed.

THREE

AT THE TOP OF THE PYRAMID THERE ARE THE INNOVATORS.

The first kid to keep her wallet on a big chunky chain. The first to wear way-too-big pants on purpose. To wash jeans in acid, stick a safety pin in something, or wear a hooded sweatshirt inside a leather jacket. The mythical first guy who wore his baseball cap *backward*.

When you meet them, most Innovators don't look that cool, not in the sense of fashionable, anyway. There's always something off about them. Like they're uncomfortable with the world. Most Innovators are actually Logo Exiles, trying to get by with the twelve pieces of clothing that are never in or out of style.

Except, like Jen's laces, there's always one thing that stands out on an Innovator. Something new.

Next level down the pyramid are the Trendsetters.

The Trendsetter's goal is to be the *second* person in the world to catch the latest disease. They watch carefully for innovations, always ready to jump on board. But more importantly, other people watch them. Unlike the Innovators, they *are* cool, so when they pick up an innovation, it *becomes* cool. A Trendsetter's most important job is gatekeeper, the filter that separates out real Innovators from those crazy people wearing garbage bags. (Although I've heard that in the 1980s, there were some Trendsetters who actually started wearing garbage bags. No comment.)

Below them are the Early Adopters.

Adopters always have the latest phone, the latest music player plugged into their ear, and they're the guys who download the trailer a year before the movie comes out. (As they grow older, Early Adopters' closets fill up with dinosaur media: Betamax videos, laser discs, eight-track tapes.) They test and tweak the trend, softening the edges. And one vital difference from Trendsetters: Early Adopters saw their stuff in a magazine first, not on the street.

Further down we have the Consumers. The people who have to see a product on TV, placed in two movies, fifteen magazine ads, and on a giant rack in the mall before saying, "Hey, that's pretty cool."

At which point it's not.

Last are the Laggards. I kind of like them. Proud in their mullets and feathered-back hair, they resist all change, or at least all change since they got out of high school. And once every ten years they suffer the uncomfortable realization that their brown leather jackets with big lapels have become, briefly, cool.

But they bravely tuck in their Kiss T-shirts and soldier on.

The unspoken rule was that Mandy's meetings were for Trendsetters. Or at least people who had been Trendsetters before Mandy hired them. Once you get paid for being trendy, who knows what you are?

A cool hunter? Market researcher? Scam artist?

A big joke?

But Jen was no joke, whether she got fifty bucks for her opinion or not. She was an Innovator. And, as I should have expected, she had committed the original sin of having uttered an original thought.

"Did I get you in trouble?" she asked on the street.

"Nah," I said. (*Nah* is Hunter-speak for *yes*.)

"Come on. Mandy was about to spit her pacifier."

I smiled at the image. "Okay, sure. You got me in trouble."

Jen sighed, eyes dropping to the gum-spotted street. "That always happens."

"What always happens?"

"I say the wrong thing." Sadness had settled into Jen's voice, which I couldn't allow.

I took a rant-sized breath. "You mean, whenever you wind up hanging out with some new crowd and they're all agreeing with each other—about the new movie they all think is great, or the band they all love, or whatever is most recently super-cool—you find yourself uncontrollably saying that it's actually crap? (Just because it is.) And suddenly they're all staring at you?"

Jen stopped right in front of the NBA store, openmouthed, framed by the merciless windowscape of team logos. I squinted in the glare.

"I guess so, yeah," she said. "I mean, *exactly*."

I smiled. I'd known a few Innovators in my day. It wasn't the easiest thing in the world to be. "And so your friends don't know what to do with you. So you shut up about it, right?"

"Well, that's the thing." She turned, and we kept walking downtown through the post-work crowd. "I never really got the shut-up-about-it part."

"Good for you."

"Which is how I got you in trouble, Hunter."

"So what? It's not like they can fix the ad with a re-edit. And it's too late to reshoot the whole thing. It would be worse if you'd said the white guy's tie was too wide. Then they'd actually have to do something."

"Oh, that makes me feel better."

"Jen, you shouldn't feel bad about this. You were the only one up there saying anything interesting. We've all done a hundred of those tastings. Maybe we've gone soft."

"Yeah, and maybe there was an MBWF thing going on in that conference room, too."

"There was?" I looked up at the skyscraper still hanging over us, and my memory flashed through all the faces, all the neighborhoods, cool groups, and constituencies represented at the tasting. I slotted each participant into his or her place on the cool Venn diagram.

Jen was right: the whole focus group had been one big missing-black-woman formation.

"I hadn't even noticed."

"Really?"

"Really." I had to smile. "That makes it even better that you spoke up. Maybe it's not what Mandy wanted to hear, but it's what she needs to hear."

Jen was silent as we took the stairs down into the subway, swiped our cards to make the turnstiles turn.

On the platform we faced each other, close in the rush-hour crowd. Around us were guys with their jackets over one arm in the summer heat and women who'd changed into sneakers with their office attire. (I always wonder: who was the Innovator on *that* one? How many ankles and arches has she saved?) Jen was still looking down, and I watched her expression shifting, her furrowed brow and green eyes mobilized by another internal debate. I had the stray thought that she probably made silly faces at little kids on the subway when their parents weren't watching and was really good at it.

She crinkled her nose in the hot smelly air. "But didn't you just say it won't make any difference?"

I shrugged. "Not for 'Don't Walk.' But maybe next time—"

My phone rang. (Down in the subway! At the risk of product place-ment, those guys in Finland do make good phones.)

shugrrl, said the display.

That was fast, I thought.

And standing there, pretty sure I was about to get fired, a funny thing happened. I found myself not caring about the job, the money, or the free shoes, but really angry that it was happening right in front of Jen and would make her feel crappy all over again to have cost me my biggest client.

"Hi, Mandy."

"Just got off the conference call. The ad airs this weekend, no changes."

"Congratulations."

"I told the client about what you and your friend said."

I started to open my mouth to say it hadn't been *my* idea at all. But that wouldn't have done any good. So I swallowed the words.

"They were intrigued," Mandy said flatly.

A train went by on the other track, and the conversation took a ten-second pause. Jen was watching me carefully, still with the bad-smell expression on her face. I mimed confusion for her.

The train rattled away into its hole.

"Intrigued as in pissed off? Intrigued as in hit-man hiring?"

"Intrigued as in interested, Hunter. They were glad to see some origi-nal thinking."

"Hey, Mandy, no reason to get personal. I just take pictures."

"I mean it. They were interested in what you said."

"Not interested enough to change the ad."

"No, Hunter. Not interested enough to reshoot a two-million-dollar ad. But there's this other thing they want your help with, an issue that actually needs some original thinking."

"It does?" I gave Jen a puzzled look. "What kind of issue?"

"It just popped up last week. It's sort of weird, Hunter. A big deal. You have to see for yourself. And you've got to keep it secret. How's tomorrow?"

"Uh, I guess it's all right. But it wasn't really me who—"

"Meet me at eleven-thirty in Chinatown, Lispenard and Church, just below Canal."

"Okay."

"And bring your new friend, of course. Don't be late."

Mandy disconnected. I dropped the phone into my pocket.

Jen cleared her throat. "So, I got you fired, didn't I?"

"No, I don't think so." I tried to imagine Mandy meeting me in Chinatown and whacking me over the head, dropping me in the Hudson sealed in concrete. "No, definitely not."

"What did she say?"

"I think we got promoted."

"We?"

I nodded, finding another smile on my face. "Yeah, we. Doing anything tomorrow?"

FOUR

"DID YOU WASH YOUR HANDS?"

My father has asked me that question at breakfast every day since I could talk. Probably before that. He's an epidemiologist, which means he studies epidemics and spends a lot of time looking at terrifying graphs of how diseases spread. These graphs, which pretty much all look the same—like a fighter jet taking off—make him worry a lot about germs.

"Yes, I washed my hands." I try to say this in exactly the same way every morning, like a robot. But my dad doesn't get the point.

"I'm glad to hear it."

My mom offered a tiny smile, pouring me some coffee. She's a perfume designer, someone who builds complicated smells out of simple ones. Her designs wind up in stores on Fifth Avenue, and I think I once caught a whiff of one on Hillary Hyphen. Which was disturbing.

"Doing anything today, Hunter?" she asked.

"Thought I'd go to Chinatown."

"Oh, is it *cool* in Chinatown these days?"

Okay. My parents don't really get my job. Not at all. Like most parents, they don't get cool. In fact, they don't actually *believe* in cool. They think it's all a big joke, like in those old movies where some guy scratches his armpit on a dance floor and everyone follows along until armpit scratching becomes a new dance craze. Yeah, right.

My parents like to emphasize the word *cool* when asking me what's going on, as if saying the word in an annoying tone will help me see through its inherent shallowness. Or maybe it's just that cool is a foreign language to them both and, like rude tourists, they think that shouting will get them understood.

But they do sign the stack of release forms I leave them every week. (Because I'm a minor, they have to give permission before multinationals pick my brain.) And they *seem* not to mind the free clothes, phones, and other electronics that show up in the mail.

"I don't know, Mom. My guess is that some of Chinatown is cool and some isn't. I'm not hunting, just meeting a friend."

"Anyone we know?"

"Her name's Jen."

My father put down his terrifying graph and raised an eyebrow. Mom raised both eyebrows.

"She's not my girlfriend or anything," I said, making a terrible mistake.

"Oh, she's not?" Dad said, half smiling. "Why do you mention that?"

I groaned. "Because you had a look on your face."

"What kind of look?"

"I just met her yesterday."

"Wow," Mom said. "You really do like her, don't you?"

I simultaneously shrugged and rolled my eyes, sending a somewhat unclear message. I hoped Dad would chalk up any redness in my face to sudden onset of West Nile fever.

My parents and I are really close, but they have this annoying idea that I'm hiding huge swaths of my romantic life from them. Which would be fine, if there were huge swaths to hide. Even medium-sized swaths.

They sat in patient silence as I cowered behind my coffee cup, waiting for a response from me. Catastrophically, all I managed to come up with was . . .

"Yeah, she's really cool."

Jen was already there, wearing non-brand, not-too-baggy jeans, the same rising-sun-laced runners as the day before, and a black T-shirt. A very classic look.

For a moment she didn't see me. Hands in pockets, leaning against a lamppost, she was checking out the street. The block of Lispenard where Mandy was meeting us was wedged between Chinatown and Tribeca, part industrial and part tourist-land. The Friday morning traffic was mostly delivery trucks. Design firms and restaurants occupied the ground floors, their signs in both Chinese and English. A few places were boarded up, and patches of cobblestones showed through the asphalt, revealing the true age of the neighborhood. These streets had first been laid down by the Dutch in the 1600s.

All the buildings around us were six stories tall. Most structures in Manhattan are six stories. Any smaller, they're not worth building. Any taller and by law you have to put in an elevator. Six-story buildings are the black T-shirt of New York architecture.

I called Jen's name when she spotted me, to which she said, "I can't believe I'm doing this."

"Doing what?"

"Coming down here as some kind of . . . *cool maven*."

I laughed. "Just say the words *cool maven* a couple more times and you won't have to worry about being one."

She rolled her eyes. "You know what I mean, Hunter."

"Actually, I don't know why we're down here any more than you do. Mandy was being all mysterious."

Jen looked down at the sidewalk, where an advertisement for some new bar had been spray painted. "But she wanted me along, right?"

"You were specifically mentioned."

"But I thought I messed everything up."

"Messing things up takes talent. Like I said yesterday, you've got a good eye. Mandy wants us to look at something."

"To see if it's *cool?*"

Apparently it was going to be one of those days when people said that word to me a lot. I put my hands up in surrender. "She just said she needed some original thinking. That's all I know."

"Original thinking?" Jen's shoulders twitched, as if her black T-shirt had shrunk in the wash. "Don't you ever think your job is kind of weird?"

I shrugged. That's what I usually do when people ask me philosophical questions about cool hunting.

But Jen didn't buy the shrug. "You know what I mean, don't you?"

"Look, Jen, most jobs are weird. My dad studies people sneezing on each other, and my mom makes smells for a living. People get paid for writing down gossip about movie stars, or judging cat shows, or selling pork-belly futures. And I'm not even sure what pork-belly futures are."

Jen raised an eyebrow. "Aren't they an option to buy pork bellies in the future at a certain price?"

I opened my mouth and found it empty of sound. This was my stock speech, and no one had ever called me on the pork-belly-futures thing before.

"My dad's a broker," she apologized.

"So tell me: why anyone would want to buy pork bellies *at all?*"

"I have no idea."

Saved. "What I mean is, if people get paid for all that stuff, why shouldn't someone get paid to figure out what's cool?"

Jen spread her hands. "Shouldn't it just . . . *be* cool?"

"Like have a special glow or something?"

"No, but if something's really cool, shouldn't people figure that out on their own? Why should they need 'Don't Walk' ads or magazines or trend spotters to tell them?"

"Because most people *aren't* cool."

"How do *you* know?"

"Look around you."

She did. The guy walking past was wearing a shirt five sizes too big (innovated by gangbangers to hide guns in their waistbands), shorts down below his knees (innovated by surfers to keep their thighs from getting sunburned), and oversized shoes (innovated by skaters to save their feet from injury). Together all of these once-practical ideas made the guy look like he'd been hit by a shrink ray and was about to disappear into his clothes screaming, *"Help me!"* in an ever-tinier voice.

Jen had to grin. Saved again.

"That guy needs our help," I said softly.

"That guy will *never* be cool. But a lot of people are getting rich off him trying. That's his money we made yesterday."

I sighed, looking up at the thin slice of sky, and noticed the weathered, faded American flags that hung from the fire escapes, rippling slowly in the breeze. They'd all been hung on the same day, without any ads telling people they had to.

Jen was silent, probably thinking I was mad at her.

But I wasn't. I was contemplating 1918.

Because of my dad I know all about 1918, the year there was a *really* nasty flu. It swept across every country in the world. It killed more people than World War I. A *billion* people got it, almost a third of everyone alive back then.

And you know what's really amazing? The virus didn't spread over the radio, and you didn't get it from watching TV or reading the side of a bus. No one was hired to spread it. Everyone who contracted the disease got it from shaking hands with, or getting sneezed on by, someone else who had it, right? So in one year just about everyone in the world had shaken hands with someone who had shaken hands with someone who had shaken hands with Patient Zero (which is what they call Innovators in the crazy world of epidemiology).

So imagine that instead of sneezing germs, all those people had been saying to each other, "Wow, this new breath mint is great! Want one?" In just a year about a billion people would be using that new breath mint without anyone ever spending a dime on advertising.

Kind of makes you think.

The uncomfortable silence stretched out for a while, and I found myself annoyed at my parents. If they hadn't been bugging me about work this morning, I wouldn't have lost my cool with Jen. She had a perfectly valid point about cool hunting—it's just that I get tired of having the same argument with my parents every day, and with other people, and with myself.

I tried to think of something to say, but all I could think about was the 1918 flu, which didn't seem like a scintillating topic of conversation. Sometimes I hate my brain.

Jen finally broke the silence.

"Maybe she's not coming."

I checked the time on my phone. Mandy was ten minutes late, which was not like Mandy. We're talking about someone who carries a clipboard.

Jen was looking down the street toward the nearest subway stop, and I got the unpleasant idea that she was thinking about leaving.

"Yeah, sorry. I'll call her." I scrolled up *shugrrl* and pressed send. Six rings later I got Mandy's voice mail.

"Must be on the subway," I said, about to leave a message, but Jen reached out one hand, touching me on the wrist.

"Hang up and call her again."

"What?"

"Wait a second." She watched a truck pass, then nodded at the phone. "Hang up and call again."

"Okay." I shrugged—that's Innovators for you—and pressed send.

Jen cocked her head, then took a few steps toward the wall of plywood that surrounded a derelict building next to us. She put her hands on the wood and leaned close to it, like she was doing a psychic reading of the layers of graffiti and posters.

Again six rings.

"Uh, Mandy," I said to the voice mail, "you said this morning, right? We're here; let us know where you are."

Jen turned around, a strange look on her face.

"So, let me guess," she said. "Despite all her cool hunting, Mandy has really Top 40 taste in music."

"Uh, yeah," I said. Maybe Jen *was* psychic. "Mandy pretty much only listens to . . ." I named a certain 1970s Swedish mega-group whose name is a four-letter word, definitely both band and brand and therefore banned from this book.

"I thought so," Jen said. "Come here. And redial."

I stood next to her and pressed send yet again.

And through the shaky plywood wall we heard tinny cell-phone tones playing a certain unforgettable ditty.

"Take a chance on me. . . ."

FIVE

"HELLO?" I POUNDED ON THE WOOD. "MANDY!"

We waited. No response.

I redialed once more to make sure.

"Take a chance on me . . ." dribbled out from behind the spray paint and advertising covering the plywood barrier.

"Okay," Jen said. "Mandy's phone is in there."

Neither of us asked the obvious question: So where was Mandy? Somewhere else altogether? Inside but unconscious? Something worse than unconscious?

Jen found a spot where two pieces of the plywood were chained together like double doors and pulled them apart as far as the fat padlock allowed. Shielding her eyes, she peered through the narrow gap.

"One more time, maestro."

I pressed send, and the little tune repeated. The refrain was starting to drive me crazy, even more than it usually did.

"There's a phone flashing in there," Jen said. "But that's all I can see."

We backed into the street, getting a better look at the derelict building. The upper-floor windows were bricked up with cinder blocks, dead gray eyes staring down at us. A coil of razor wire topped the plywood barrier around the ground floor, the fluttering remains of plastic bags collected on its spikes. An arm's length of unspooled cassette tape was caught on the wire, the light wind making it undulate and flicker in the sun.

The building must have been abandoned for months. Maybe years. I mean, *cassette* tape?

"No way in," I said, but found that I wasn't talking to anyone.

Jen was next door, already up the front-stoop stairs and stabbing buzzer buttons at random. The intercom popped, and a garbled voice queried her.

"Delivery," she said loudly and clearly.

The door buzzed. She opened it, stuck her foot in, and waved at me impatiently to follow.

I swallowed. This was what I got for hanging out with an Innovator.

But as I may have mentioned or implied, I'm a Trendsetter. Our purpose in life is to be second in line, to follow. I bounded up the steps and grabbed the outer door just as the buzz came again and she pushed her way inside.

At the top of the third flight of stairs a tousle-haired man was waiting, his head sticking out his door. He looked at us sleepily.

"The delivery guy's right behind us," Jen said, and kept on climbing.

A half flight up from the sixth floor we found the door to the roof. A cagelike contraption sealed us off from the last flight of stairs, the usual precaution to keep people from getting into the building from topside. Of course, the door could be opened from the inside in case of fire, but across the push bar a big red sticker was plastered:

WARNING: ALARM WILL SOUND IF OPENED

I panted, recovering from the climb, relieved that we couldn't go any farther. Even if Jen was an Innovator, breaking into an abandoned building wasn't my idea of cool. Having thought about it for a minute, I was figuring we should call the police. Mandy must have been mugged, her phone tossed into the derelict building.

But where was she?

"You know the trick to these alarms?" Jen asked, placing one finger lightly on the push bar.

My relief faded. "There's a trick?"

"Yeah." She pushed, and an earsplitting screech filled the stairway, loud enough to be heard by everyone in Chinatown.

"They stop on their own eventually!" she shouted above the alarm, and darted through the door.

I covered my ears and looked back down the stairs, imagining annoyed tenants emerging from every door. And then I followed Jen.

The roof was tar, painted silver to keep the summer sun from boiling the people who lived on the top floor. We pounded across it, the alarm still shrieking like a huge and angry teakettle behind us.

The next building over, the one we were trying to break into (correction: that *Jen* was trying to break into—I was just along for the ride), stood a bit shorter, a drop of six feet or so. She sat on the edge and jumped, landing on black and ragged tar with a thump that sounded painful.

I climbed partway down, clinging to the edge, falling the least possible distance but still managing to twist my ankle.

I scowled as I limped after Jen. It was all the client's fault. A hundred pairs of shoes and they'd never sent me a sneaker optimized for urban burglary.

The roof door of the abandoned building opened with a metal screech, hanging on one hinge like a dislocated shoulder. Behind it was a dark staircase that smelled of dust and old garbage and something as sharp and nasty as the time my parents' apartment had a dead rat in the wall.

Jen looked back at me, showing a bit of hesitation for the first time.

She opened her mouth to speak, but at that moment the alarm from the next building stopped, the silence hitting us like a hammer.

Through the ringing echoes in my ears I thought I heard an annoyed voice on the roof behind us.

"Go on," I whispered.

We went down into the darkness.

Walking around New York, looking up, I often wonder what goes on behind all those windows. Especially the empty ones.

I've been to parties in squats, old buildings taken over by enterprising homesteaders who do their own repairs. And everyone knows that crackheads and homeless people occupy abandoned buildings, inhabiting an invisible reality behind the blank windows and cinder blocks. There's this rumor that Chinatown has its own secret government, an ancient system of laws and obligations brought over from the old country, which I'd always imagined being run from inside a derelict building like this, complete with town meetings and trials and punishments meted out. Basically anything could be going on behind those blank and faceless windows.

But I never thought I'd actually be finding out for myself.

The air was difficult to breathe, baked hard by the summer sun. As Jen descended, she left dust coiling behind her in the few shafts of light. Her runners left footprints on the stairs, which made me feel better. Maybe no one ever came here. Maybe some buildings were just . . . empty.

Every floor down it got darker.

Jen stopped after three flights, waiting for our eyes to adjust, listening carefully to the silence. My ears were still ringing with the alarm screech, but as far as I could tell, no one had followed us from the building next door.

Who would do anything that crazy?

"Do you have any matches?" Jen said softly.

"No, but this works." I switched my phone to camera mode, careful to turn the bright screen away so I didn't blind myself. It shone like a little flashlight in the pitch blackness. It was a useful trick for fiddling with keys on late nights.

"Gee, is there anything that phone doesn't do?"

"It's no use against crackheads," I said. "Or officials of the Chinatown secret government."

"The what?"

"I'll tell you later."

We descended the last three flights, the phone scattering a weird blue light that gave our dancing shadows a ghostly pallor.

I darkened my phone when we reached the ground floor. Now that our eyes had adjusted, the sun streaming through gaps in the plywood shone like a row of spotlights. The ceiling was high, the whole floor stretching out unobstructed except for a few thick, square columns. What had once been store windows were now gaping rectangular holes in the wall, only plywood separating us from the street. Not even broken glass remained.

"Someone's using this floor," Jen said.

"What do you mean?"

She scuffed one shoe across the concrete next to a patch of light.

"No dust."

She was right. The sunlight revealed no coiling cloud around her shoe. The floor had recently been swept clean.

I ran my thumb to the familiar shape of the send button. A moment later the little multi-platinum tune played from a distant corner.

As we crossed, taking careful steps, I saw that the wall nearest to the flashing phone was lined with stacks of small boxes. Someone was in fact using the building for storage.

Jen knelt and picked up the phone, checking the floor around it.

"Nothing else here of Mandy's. Does she carry a purse?"

"Just a clipboard. If she got mugged, would they keep that?"

"Maybe they just tossed the phone in so she couldn't call for help."

"Maybe . . ." My voice trailed off.

Of its own accord, my hand went to the stacked boxes, pulled by magnets of familiarity and desire. I ran my fingers down the lids spaced every four inches. The boxes were a common size and shape, so familiar that I almost hadn't realized what they were at first.

Shoe boxes.

I reached up and pulled one from the top of the stack. Opened it and breathed the new-car smell of unused plastic, heard the crinkle of paper, felt plastic and rubber and string. I lifted out the pair and set them on the ground in a shaft of sunlight.

Jen gasped, and I stepped back, blinking at the sudden radiance of panels, laces, tongue, and tread. Neither of us said a word, but we both knew instantly.

They were the coolest shoes we'd ever seen.

SIX

ANTOINE HAD TOLD ME THE HISTORY OF SHOES MANY TIMES:

In the beginning, the late 1980s, the client was king. A certain basketball player (whose name basically became a brand) made them king. An industry was transformed, and shoes grew air pumps and Velcro straps, gel chambers and light-emitting diodes. New models came out seasonally, then monthly, and Antoine started buying two pairs, one for wearing and one for saving, like comic-book collectors with their plastic bags.

And of course that bubble burst. People wanted shoes, not spaceships. Innovators began to search suburban malls for the humble sneakers of their childhood. Trendsetters demanded whole new categories of shoes: for skating, snowboarding, surfing, walking, running, and every other sport (parachutists probably have their own shoes), and to save all those secretaries time, hybrids appeared, dressy on top and rubber in the sole.

The client—with its flashy, gimmicky, jump-shooting shoes—faded. The world it had dominated disappeared, broken down into a patchwork of tribes and cliques and niches, like some neighborhood controlled by a different gang on every block.

But the pair in front of us recalled the oldies in Antoine's lovingly stacked boxes in the Bronx, those ancient, golden, simple days. Not spaceships—just shoes with insane confidence, vitality, and flair.

Sheer cool.

◇　◆　◇

"Wow," Jen said.

"I know." Acting on instinct, I pointed my phone and took a picture.

"Wow," she repeated.

I reached out, and my hand glowed in the shaft of sunlight, as if the shoes were infecting me with their magic. The texture of the panels was something I'd never felt before, as rough and pliable as canvas but with the silvery shine of metal. The laces flowed through my fingers as softly as ropes made out of silk. The eyelets seemed to have tiny spokes that turned when I flexed the shoe, using the same effect as those 3-D postcards that change when you look at them from different directions.

But the individual flourishes weren't what made the shoes incredible. It was the way they called to me to put them on, the way I was sure I could fly if I was wearing a pair. The way I needed to buy them *now*.

A way I hadn't felt since I was ten.

"So this is what Mandy wanted us to see."

"No kidding," I said. "The client must be keeping this a total secret."

"The client? Look again, Hunter."

She was pointing at a circle of plastic set into the tongue, where the client's logo stood out bright white and proud. With my brain gradually recovering from its dazzlement, I saw what Jen had spotted right away. The logo—one of the world's best-known symbols, up there with the white flag of surrender and the golden arches—had been cut through with a diagonal line in bright red.

Like a no-smoking sign. Like a no-whatever sign. The bar sinister, a symbol of prohibition also recognized around the world.

It was an anti-logo.

"Bootlegs," I murmured. That was another thing that went on in the shadows of Chinatown. In rows of small, discreet shops on Canal Street you could buy watches and jeans, handbags and shirts, wallets and belts, all with the labels of famous designers sewn onto them by hand. All cheap and fake. Some were laughably crude, some pretty much passable, and a few required an eye as expert as Hillary Hyphen's to spot the telltale wrong stitch.

But I'd never seen any bootleg that was *better* than the original.

"Not exactly bootlegs, Hunter. I mean, it's saying right up front what it's not."

"True. I guess a bootlegger wouldn't do that."

"But who *would* do something like that? What's the point of a non-bootleg bootleg?"

"I don't know," I said. "They're so *good.* Like the perfect shoe the client never made."

Jen shook her head. "But Mandy called us here. Does she work for anyone besides the client?"

"No. She's exclusive." I frowned. "Maybe this really is their shoe. Maybe they have this master plan of rebranding as the opposite of themselves. Or maybe these are supposed to look like bootlegs when they're not. And after these get *too* popular, which they will, the client will absorb the backlash and become cool again. Maybe they're ironic bootlegs."

Confused? Trust me, it was making my head hurt, and it's my job to think this way.

"That's so insane," Jen said. "Or pure genius. Or something."

"Something *really* cool."

"So where's Mandy?"

"Oh, yeah." Mandy was still missing. What did that mean?

Jen and I sat there, sharing a moment of befuddlement, contemplation, and the thirsty pleasure of simply looking.

Then I heard a noise somewhere in the darkness behind us.

I tugged my eyes away from the shoe, looked up at Jen. She'd heard it too.

Glancing into the dark, I realized that my night vision had been wiped out by staring at the sunlit shoe. I was blinded but guessed that whoever was down there with us could see perfectly.

"Oh, shit," I said.

With a soft rustle of paper Jen picked up the shoes and quickly laced them together. She draped them around her neck.

I stood up and realized that one foot had gone to sleep. Not surprising. I could have happily died of starvation, staring at those shoes.

Little lights danced at the corners of my vision, rods and cones trying frantically to get back online and help me see again. A shape moved in the blackness between us and the stairs, someone big and graceful. Absolutely silent.

"Hello?" I said, my voice cracking in manly fashion.

The figure stopped moving and faded back into the dark. For a moment I was convinced it had been a hallucination.

Then Jen made her move.

She kicked one of the pieces of chained plywood, opening the gap wide for a blinding second, the sunlight streaming in behind me. It revealed a big guy with a shaved head—intimidating but less terrifying than the phantom I had imagined—covering his eyes against the glare.

"Run!" Jen shouted, and I bolted forward just in time for the tower of falling shoe boxes, her next brilliant move, to miss me. Mostly. They scattered into my path, and my own suddenly unspeakably lame shoes crunched into their virgin cardboard in a way that caused me pain. (Antoine had always taught me to prize the original box as highly as the shoe.) But I managed to get past the guy, arriving at the stairs just behind Jen.

We ran upward, pounding the steps. Jen slowly pulled away from me, and I heard our pursuer coming up behind. I ran blindly, clawing at the dirty stairs with my hands to pull myself up faster, bouncing off the walls as the flights turned in a slow clockwise circle, my twisted ankle throbbing with every step.

After four stories I was panting, and he was close enough that I could tell he wasn't breathing hard at all.

Fingers grasped at my ankle on the last flight but slipped off, the grip not firm enough to bring me down.

I burst out into the sun, blinked away the blinding light, and faced the six-foot climb between me and the next roof. Jen was already standing atop it, and I wondered if her rising-sun laces gave her special powers of running and jumping.

"Hunter, duck!" she yelled.

I did.

The coolest shoes in the world passed over my head, tied into orbit around each other, spinning like a bola. I heard a grunt and a thump as they wrapped themselves around my pursuer's feet and brought him down, as heavy as a sack of doorknobs.

If it hadn't happened so fast, I'm sure I would have said, "Don't save me. Save the shoes!"

But instead I scrambled up the wall and saw Jen already pulling on the cage door of the next building.

"It's locked!" she cried, running farther down the block, disappearing as she jumped down to a lower roof. I followed in a limping run.

Three buildings later we found an open roof door and made it down to the street and into a cab.

Which is when I realized I had dropped my phone somewhere back in the darkness.

SEVEN

"MY PHONE!"

The usual panic reaction: as if electrocuted, my body stiffened in the back of the cab, hands plunging farther into my pockets, down to the domain of lint and pennies.

But the marvelous Finnish phone didn't magically reappear down there in the fluff. It was gone.

"You dropped it?"

"Yeah." I remembered scrambling in the dark, using my hands to claw myself up the stairs. I'd never put it back into my pocket.

"Damn. I was hoping you got a picture of that guy."

I looked at Jen in disbelief. "Not quite. I was more focused on the running away."

"Well, sure. The running away was a priority." She grinned. "The running away was cool."

My face may have indicated disagreement.

"Come on, Hunter. You don't mind a little running, do you?"

"I don't mind running, Jen. I do mind running *for my life*. Next time we break into some place, let's just—"

"What? Take a vote first?"

I took a deep breath, letting the sway of the taxi calm me.

"Let's just not." Then another groan. "I had a picture of the shoes."

"Damn," she agreed.

We were silent for a moment, thinking of that perfect balance of understated style, slow-burning desirability, and coffee-spitting, jaw-dropping eye candy that was the shoes.

"They can't be as good as we remember," I said.

"Nice try. They were."

"Crap." I checked my pockets again. Still empty. "No phone, no shoes, no Mandy. This is a total disaster."

"Not quite, Hunter."

Jen held up what looked like my phone, except it was the wrong color.

Of course. It was Mandy's. She had the same model as I did (but with the red translucent clip-on cover). She was a fierce Early Adopter, and, like me, she used the phone for business. Just the day before, I'd phoned her my picture of Jen's shoelaces.

"Well, that's something."

Jen nodded. There's a lot you can find out from someone's phone.

She began to poke her way through the menu, squinting at the glowing screen. The little beeps gave me a creepy feeling, like going through someone's pockets.

"Shouldn't we call the police or something?"

"And tell them what?" Jen said. "That Mandy missed an appointment? Don't you watch cop shows? She's an adult. She can't be a missing person for twenty-four hours."

"But we found her phone. Isn't that suspicious?"

"Maybe she dropped it."

"But what about the guy who chased us? What about the shoes?"

"Yeah, we could tell the cops about that. About how we broke into an abandoned building and saw the world's most amazing shoes. And then a crazy bald guy appeared, and we ran away. That story should do wonders for our credibility."

I was silent for a moment, out of arguments but still not comfortable. "Jen, Mandy's my friend."

She turned to me, thought for a moment, then nodded.

"You're right. We should try the cops. But if they do listen to us, they'll take Mandy's phone away."

"So?"

Jen turned back to the little screen. "Maybe she took some pictures."

We stopped the cab, paid for it, and found a coffee shop of the musty-living-room variety: old couches, high-speed Internet access, and strong coffee, which came in cups the size of bowls.

Even before we walked through the door, I noticed Jen's bracelet sparkling.

"What's that?"

She smiled. "It's a Wi-Fi detector. You know, so you don't have to boot up your computer to see if there's wireless in the house."

I gave the Nod. I'd seen them in magazines, useful for detecting which coffee shops and hotels offered wireless service, but wearing the gadget as jewelry was pure Innovator.

We claimed a couch and huddled over Mandy's phone, our heads almost touching to align our eyes to the pixels of its little screen. Not really designed for two viewers, that phone, but I wasn't complaining. That close, I could smell Jen's hair stuff, a hint of vanilla cutting through the musty couch and ground coffee. Her shoulder was warm against mine.

"Something wrong?" she asked.

"Uh, no." Memo to self: It's uncool to be overwhelmed by casual contact.

I brought up the camera software, my fingers gliding over the cruelly familiar interface. (Maybe the Finlanders would send me another one.) The menu showed five pictures, displayed in the order they were taken. One thumb click later, a fuzzy orange face filled the screen.

"That's Mandy's cat, Muffin. He eats cockroaches."

"Useful beast."

Next click a young Latina woman appeared, smiling and fending off the camera, breakfast in the lower third of the screen.

"Cassandra, her roommate. Or girlfriend—no one's sure."

"That would be girlfriend," Jen said. "No one bothers to take a picture of their roommate."

"Maybe not, but when I first got my phone, I was taking pictures of my sock drawer."

She gripped my arm. "How will you live without it?"

"I don't call it living."

I clicked again. A guy wearing a black beret, maybe a little floppier than the last beret craze. A cool-hunting picture.

"Logo's too big, band's too tight," Jen said. "And no berets in summer."

"And that shirt looks way Uptown," I said. "Not the sort of thing you'd see in Chinatown." I checked the picture's time stamp. "She took it yesterday."

The next picture brought a small gasp from Jen. It was a shoe, *Jen's* shoe, the rising-sun laces instantly recognizable. I could even see the hexagonal pattern of the East River Park promenade.

"Is that . . . ? That's the picture you—"

"Uh, yeah, I sent it to Mandy," I confessed.

She pulled away, turned to me with narrowed eyes. I felt the musty-couch intimacy that had built up between us swirling away.

"You're not still confused about what I do for a living, are you?"

"No. But it's just sinking in." She looked down at her laces. "I'm trying to figure out if I feel violated."

"Uh, try flattered, maybe?"

"Hang on—what exactly was Mandy going to do with it?"

"Take a look at it? Maybe pass it up the food chain." I cleared my throat, deciding to go for broke. "Possibly use it in an ad or two. Put it into mass production. Make it available in every mall in America. Run your laces into the ground, basically."

I saw questions crossing Jen's face, the familiar ones: *Am I being ripped off? Is this a compliment? Am I secretly famous? When do I get my percentage?*

And of course: *Is this guy an asshole or what?*

"Wow," she said, after a long, awkward moment. "I always wondered how that happened."

"How what happened?"

"How cool stuff became uncool so fast. Like one day I see a couple of *cholos* wearing aprons on the street. Then ten minutes later they're in Kmart. But I guess I didn't realize what an industry it was. I figured at least some of it happened naturally."

I sighed. "It does, sometimes. But usually nature gets a helping hand."

"Right. Like sunsets with lots of pollution."

"Or genetically engineered bananas."

She laughed, glancing at her laces again. "Okay, I'll get over it. You sure know how to flatter a girl."

I grinned happily—with that sudden and complete failure of irony detection that occurs when irony most needs to be detected—while questions rattled through my brain: Was she really flattered? Was I a fraud? Had I blown everything? What was "everything," anyway?

To cover my confusion, I clicked to the next picture.

The shoe.

My brain settled, focused by the beauty. We huddled again, pressed close for the best view on the little screen. The picture was minuscule, badly lit, agonizingly blurry, but the elegant lines and textures were somehow still there.

We sat for a solid minute, sucking in the beauty, while around us trancy coffee shop music played, cappuccinos roared into being, and would-be writers wrote novels set in coffee shops. In the bliss our shoulders practically melted together, and I felt forgiven for stealing Jen's shoelace mojo. The bootleg-or-maybe-not shoe was just that good.

Finally we pulled away from each other, blinking and breathless, as if we'd shared a kiss instead of a cell-phone screen.

"When did she take that?" Jen asked.

I checked the time stamp. "Yesterday. A couple of hours before the tasting."

"They look like they're on a desk."

"That's her office, I think." The shoe was sitting on a paper-strewn expanse not unlike Mandy's desk up in the client's Midtown tower.

"Which means . . . What does it mean?"

"Search me. Last picture?"

She looked at the screen for another greedy moment before nodding.

I clicked. It was a picture of nothing. Or something terrible.

Dark and blurry, an abstract gash of light across one corner. Shades of grays all mottled together like a camo pattern. It was either an accidental photo from the bottom of Mandy's pocket, the visual equivalent of those random calls your phone makes when it gets bored, or it was a picture of Mandy being mugged, kidnapped, or worse. Maybe she'd tried to record what had happened to her, then thrown the phone away, hoping someone would find it.

But I couldn't make much out.

"Hang on." Jen pulled my hand closer, the phone almost to her eye. "There's a face. . . ." She turned away, shaking her head. "Maybe. You try."

I took a closer look. Somewhere in the swirl of indifferent grays, there was something recognizable. A thing that my brain would, if I let it, twist slowly into a face.

Which freaked me out and also gave me a headache.

I checked the time stamp. "This was taken about an hour ago."

"A little before eleven? That's about when I showed up."

"But you didn't see anything?"

Jen shook her head and stared at the tiny screen again.

"You can get these pictures onto a computer, right? Maybe there's some kind of software we can run to make this clearer."

I nodded. "I've got a friend. She does special effects."

"What about the cops, Hunter?"

I took a deep breath. Lexa lived only two blocks away. It wouldn't take long.

"They can wait."

EIGHT

"YOU HAVE TO TAKE YOUR SHOES OFF," I TOLD JEN OUTSIDE
Lexa's door.

"Okay." She bent to tug at a lace. "A Zen thing?"

"No, a clean thing."

Lexa Legault vacuumed her apartment every day with a small jet engine, leaving it as spotless as a biotech lab. I always felt like she should have asked her guests to wear white jumpsuits and masks, but I guess that would've been overkill. Lexa (short for Alexandra) didn't make her own microchips yet.

What she did make was her own computers, which spent their lives with their guts exposed, in a state of constantly being tinkered with. In Lexa's apartment, dust was a Very Bad Thing.

I'd already buzzed from downstairs, but it wasn't until I gave the special our-shoes-are-off knock that the door opened.

Lexa was dressed in immaculate khakis and a tight pink T-shirt, a handheld clipped to her belt. She had all the hallmarks of geek-girl beauty: a shy smile, chunky glasses, short hair framing elfin features, and the fashion sense of a Japanese teenager. Her look was as effortless and clean as those women that fashion designers draw with just a few sweeping lines.

When I'd first met Lexa, I'd spent several months cultivating a massive crush on her until the terrible moment when she'd mentioned that one of the things she liked about me was how much I reminded her of herself—back when she was younger and not so boringly together. I never let on, of course, but *ouch*.

"Hi, Hunter." She hugged me, pulled back, still looking over my shoulder. "Oh, hey . . ."

"Jen," I supplied.

"Yeah," nodding slowly, "I liked what you said yesterday, Jen. Very cool."

That brought a sheepish smile, one I liked more every time I saw it. "Thanks."

We slipped into the apartment, and Lexa closed the door immediately behind us to fend off any dust swirling in our wake.

I handed her the cup of coffee we'd brought as an offering. She always said her brain was nothing but a machine for turning coffee into special effects.

Jen took in the high-tech splendor, her eyes widening as they adjusted to the darkness. Hardly any sunlight leaked in through the heavy curtains (like dust, sunlight was a Bad Thing), but the apartment glowed around us. All of Lexa's furniture was made out of the stainless steel used in restaurant kitchens. The metal glittered with the scattered red and green eyes of gadgets recharging: a couple of cell phones, an MP3 player, three laptops, an electric toothbrush by the kitchen sink. (Despite all the coffee, Lexa's teeth were as clean as her apartment.) And of course there were several computers running screen savers, coiling blobs of light that reflected throughout the room. Jen's Wi-Fi bracelet joined in the sparkling, excited by the heavy wireless traffic. Lexa noticed the bracelet and gave it the Nod, and I felt obscurely pleased by this sign of approval.

Steel shelves lined the walls, filled with memory chips and disk drives and cables, all of these spare parts coded with colored stickers. The top shelves were lined with about a dozen of those electric fireplaces with fake glowing embers, so that the ceiling pulsed with a rosy light.

Sometimes there is a very fine line between being cool and being a crank. Whether you're one or the other depends on the overall effect. Lexa's apartment always filled me with a sense of calm, a room full of candles but without the fire hazard. It was like being inside a huge meditating head. Maybe it was a Zen thing after all.

Making good money also helps with not being a crank. Lexa was famous for her special-effects work for a certain previously mentioned movie franchise, the one involving frozen kung fu and lots of ammunition. With plenty of income, Lexa cool-hunted as a hobby, as a calling, even. Her goal in life was to influence the manufacturers of MP3 players, cell phones, and handhelds to follow the principles of good design—clean lines, ergonomic buttons, and softly pulsing lights.

"You haven't been over in a while, Hunter." She glanced at Jen, wondering if I'd been busy.

"Yeah, you know. Summer."

"Did you get my e-mail about joining SHIFT?"

"Uh, yeah."

One more word about cranks: An Innovator friend of Lexa's had this theory that uppercase was coming back in. That all the Webby kids who'd never hit the shift key in their lives (except to type an @ sign) were about to start putting capitals at the beginning of their sentences, maybe even the first letter of their names and other proper nouns. Lexa didn't really believe this seismic shift was imminent, but she desperately wanted it to be. Typographical laziness was slowly destroying our culture, according to Lexa and her pals. Inexactitude was death.

I wasn't clear on the details of the theory. But the concept behind SHIFT was that if enough Trendsetters started using capital letters in their e-mails and posts, maybe the herd would follow.

"You haven't joined up, have you?"

I cleared my throat. "I'm sort of agnostic on the whole SHIFT agenda."

"Agnostic? You mean you aren't sure if capital letters exist?" Lexa could be literal minded at times.

"No, I believe in them. I've actually seen a few. But as far as the need for a *movement* goes—"

"What are you guys talking about?"

Lexa turned to Jen, eyes alight with the prospect of a conversion. "You know how no one uses capitals anymore? Just dribbles along in lowercase, like they don't know where the sentence starts?"

"Yeah, I hate that."

Lexa's well-brushed smile was blinding in the rosy gloom. "Oh, you've got to get into SHIFT, then. What's your e-mail?"

"Um, Lexa, can I interrupt?"

She stopped, her handheld already unclipped from her belt, ready to take Jen's contact information.

"We came here about something important."

"Sure, Hunter." She reluctantly returned the tiny computer to her belt. "What's up?"

"Mandy's disappeared."

Lexa crossed her arms. "Disappeared? Define."

"She was supposed to meet us in Chinatown this morning," I said. "She didn't show."

"You tried calling her?"

"We did, which is how we found this." I held up Mandy's phone.

"It's hers," Jen said. "It was in an abandoned building near where we were supposed to meet her."

"That's a little creepy," Lexa admitted.

"More than a little," Jen said. "There's a picture on the phone. It's blurry but kind of scary. Like maybe something happened to her."

Lexa held out her hand. "May I?"

"We were hoping you would."

Using Lexa's cinematographic hardware to look at a postage-stamp digital photo was like using the space shuttle to get to the end of the street. But the results were equally earthshaking.

On Lexa's giant flat screen Mandy's last picture looked a hundred times more ominous. The gash of white that cut across one corner made sense now. It was the gap between the boards of the abandoned building, sunlight pouring through. The photo had evidently been taken from inside, only a few steps from where we'd found the phone.

"It looks like it's been unlocked," Jen said, standing. Her fingers traced a dark snake in the bright patch, a chain swinging free between the boards, the blurred shape of an open padlock hanging at one end. The gap seemed wide enough for a person to squeeze through.

"So Mandy had a key," I said. "She said she was going to show us something."

Jen pointed. "But when she opened it, somebody else was in there."

I squinted at the blotchy shape in the darkest corner of the picture. Blown up this big, it seemed less like a face, the gradients of gray more jagged, like a mob informer with his identity concealed by computer.

"What do you think, Lexa? Is that a face?"

She was also squinting. "Yeah, maybe."

"Can you do anything to clear it up?" Jen asked.

Lexa crossed her arms. "Clear it up? Define."

"Well, make it look more like a face. Like on cop shows when the FBI guys do that computer stuff to pictures?"

Lexa sighed. "Let me explain something, guys: Those scenes are rigged. You can't really make a blurry picture clearer; the information's already gone. Besides, when it comes to faces, your brains are better than any computer."

"Couldn't you give our brains a hand?" I asked.

"Look, I've created ocean waves, crashing cars, whirling asteroids. I've erased boils from movie stars' hands, made it snow and rain, even added smoke to an actress's breath after she refused to put a lit cigarette in her mouth. But you know what the hardest thing to animate is?"

Jen dared a guess. "A human face?"

"Exactly."

"Because it's so mobile?"

Lexa shook her head. "Humans aren't especially expressive. Monkeys' faces are more muscular, dogs have much bigger eyes, and cats have very emotive whiskers. Our crappy ears don't even move. What makes humans so tough to do is the audience. *We're* human, and we spend our whole lives learning to read each other's faces. We can detect a glimmer of anger on another person's face from a hundred yards through a fog bank. Our brains are machines for turning coffee into facial analysis. Take a drink and look for yourself."

I swallowed the cold dregs from my paper cup and stared at the picture. It *was* a face, I decided, and it was starting to look familiar.

"Although frankly, this might help." Lexa stood but didn't reach for the mouse. She went to the kitchen drawer and pulled out a long, thin box. With a swish and a tearing sound, she extracted a large sheet of wax paper, the kind you wrap sandwiches in. She held the translucent paper over the screen.

"Don't ever tell anyone I said this, but sometimes blurry is better than clear."

Jen and I gasped. Through the haze of the paper something recognizable had resolved.

It was the face of the man who'd come after us in the darkness. The bald head was obvious now, the heavy brow and childish lips all somehow cohering in the blur. And Lexa was right: we could read the expression perfectly, right through the wax paper and pixelization and darkness. The guy was eager, determined, totally in control.

He was coming to get Mandy, like he'd tried to get us.

We sat there for a moment in silence, paralyzed, as if he'd stepped through the screen into the room. Then a bouncy Swedish tune started to play.

Take a chance on me. . . .

Mandy's phone had come to life, its lights blinking away. Lexa took a step, lifted it to look at its little screen.

"That's funny."

"Who's calling?" I asked.

Lexa lifted an eyebrow.

"You are, Hunter."

NINE

LEXA HANDED ME THE PHONE. THE SWEDISH TUNE KEPT PLAYING, insistent and diabolical.

The readout glowed in the darkness. *Incoming call: Hunter.*

"It really is me," I said to Jen. "It's my phone calling."

"Maybe you should answer."

"Oh, yeah." I swallowed and lifted the phone to my ear. "Hello?"

"Hi, uh, I'm just calling because I found this phone. And I wanted to return it to the owner."

"Really?" My foolish heart lifted.

"Yeah, and this number was in the incoming call memory, so I figured the phone must belong to a friend of yours. Maybe you could give me the guy's name. Or his address?"

"Yeah, actually that's . . ."

My voice trailed off as I came to my senses: why did this person assume the phone's owner was a he?

"Uh, actually . . ." I looked up at the face on the screen, at arm's length now. The voice on the phone was male and sounded like a big guy.

Maybe *that* guy.

I cleared my throat. "Actually, I don't recognize this number."

"Are you sure? You just called it an hour ago. Like four times in a row."

"Uh, yeah, that was a wrong number," I said, trying to keep the tremor out of my voice. "I have no idea whose number this is."

"Oh, okay. Well, sorry to bother you . . . Shoe Girl."

The phone went dead.

Shoe Girl, he'd said. That was the name in my phone for Mandy: *shugrrl,* her instant-message handle. He knew I'd been lying.

"It was him, wasn't it?" Jen said.

I nodded, looking at the grim face on the screen. "He's calling the numbers in my memory, saying he wants to return a lost phone. He's trying to find someone who'll give him my address."

"Oh, crap," said Jen. "But no one would do that, would they?"

"I've got about a hundred numbers in that phone. Eventually someone will give him what he wants. Probably my aunt Macy in Minnesota."

"You could call your aunt," Jen said, "and all your close friends, the ones who know your address, and tell them what's going on."

"That might work if I *could* call them." I shook my head. "I don't actually keep anyone's number in my head. Without that phone, I'm toast."

"You don't back up?" asked Lexa, scandalized.

"Sure, at home." I tried to remember the last time I'd actually backed up the phone onto my computer. A boring day during Christmas vacation? "But by the time I get there and call everyone . . ."

"Okay, guys, I was just trying to help with this and not be too nosy. But this is getting weird." Lexa pointed at the screen. "How did *that* guy get your phone? And why does he care what your address is?"

"Well, after Mandy didn't show up, he did. You see, we were in this old building, and there were these . . . shoes."

"Shoes." Lexa sighed. "Why is it always shoes with you guys?"

"They were amazing," Jen said softly.

"Amazing? Define."

"Can you keep a secret?" I said.

"Sure."

"I mean, *really* keep a secret."

"Hunter, I got the script for . . ." (she named the third movie of a franchise in which a certain weight-lifting governor plays an unsmiling robot who shoots things) ". . . a year before it came out. And I didn't leak a single plot point."

"That's because there weren't any," I said. "Just don't tell anyone about this, okay? Go one picture back."

She clicked, and Mandy's picture of the shoe filled the screen. Lexa blinked, uncrossed her arms, and took a drink of her coffee. Stoking the machine.

It was grainy, jagged, the colors blotchy, but it was still the shoe.

"Wow, the client did *that?* Didn't know they had it in them."

"We're not sure," Jen said. "It's either a bootleg or some radical new marketing concept. You can't tell from this picture, but the logo has a bar sinister through it."

"It's the anti-client," I said.

Lexa smiled and gave a slow nod. The Nod. "Cool."

"Cool enough to kidnap someone over?" I asked.

"Sure, Hunter." Lexa stepped back, squinting now, blurring the jagged picture with her eyelashes. "Cool is money, and money can be worth anything. That's money's job."

It was a way that only computer geeks talked, but it made sense. Jen gave Lexa the Nod.

We sucked the memory out of Mandy's phone and made some calls.

Her office phone went to a machine, and we left the obvious "Where are you?" message. Cassandra's cell phone did likewise, and I explained that Mandy had missed a meeting and could Cassandra please call Lexa. When Mandy's home machine answered, I just hung up, not wanting to leave multiple messages all smelling of fear. Until we had something more solid, I didn't see the point in worrying Cassandra about her missing roommate/girlfriend.

Then we looked at Mandy's outgoing numbers. The last place Mandy had called was a car service, which was how she traveled since going full-time. The other outgoing calls led to the client's massive switchboards, nonspecific numbers that ended in three zeros—probably Mandy conferring with her bosses about "Don't Walk." The only other call in memory was one to her home the night before. There were no clues that she had arranged to meet anyone else besides us this morning.

But *someone* had told Mandy about the building and its mysterious contents. At least one of the client's countless execs knew more than we did.

I looked at the phone. Having just had my cell phone ripped from my life, I knew how much information was trapped inside in the tiny plastic wafer of circuitry, but there was no easy way to get it out. Machines don't give up their secrets easily.

Human beings, on the other hand, love to spill the beans. One by one, I went through the client's numbers that Mandy had stored, skipping straight past phone trees to human receptionists. Eventually one made the connection for me.

"Hello, I'm making a call on behalf of Mandy Wilkins."

"Oh, do you want Mr. Harper?"

"Uh, yes. Please."

"I'll connect you."

I waited for a moment on hold, listening to custom rap-Muzak exalting the latest big sports name who'd signed on the client's dotted line. It sucked me in just far enough that my brain got a jolt when the exec came on.

"Greg Harper. Who is this?"

"My name is Hunter Braque. I work with Mandy Wilkins. I was supposed to meet her this morning at Lispenard and Church . . . about the shoes."

"The shoes, yeah." His voice was slow, cautious. "I think she told me about bringing you in. Outside consultant, right?"

"Exactly."

"Right, I remember now. Hunter." His voice changed, sharpened by recognition. "You focused on 'Don't Walk,' didn't you? Caused all that trouble?"

"Uh, I guess that was me. Anyway, she didn't make the meeting—"

"Maybe she had second thoughts."

"Actually, I'm a bit worried. She didn't show for our meeting, but we found her phone. She's missing, sort of, and we were wondering what this was all about. The shoes, I mean."

"I can't comment about the shoes. We do a lot of shoes. This is a shoe company. I don't even know what shoes you mean."

"Listen, Mr. Harper, I saw them—"

"Saw what? You should have Mandy call me."

"But I don't know where she—"

"Have Mandy call me."

The line went dead. No Muzak, nothing. Somewhere during the call Jen and Lexa had stopped playing with the photo of the shoe to listen.

When I dropped the phone from my ear, Jen said, "What was that about?"

I'd heard many forms of corporate desperation before, the frantic tones of lost market share, crumbling stock prices, multimillion-dollar contracts with college hoop stars who weren't cutting it in the pros, the horrifying realization of not knowing what those damn kids wanted anymore. But nothing quite as panicked as Greg Harper's last words.

"I think the client is in a state of denial," I said. "But one thing's for certain: The shoes didn't come from them."

"So where did they come from?" Lexa asked.

I looked at Jen; she looked at me.

We shrugged.

TEN

ONE THING ABOUT BEING A COOL HUNTER, YOU REALIZE ONE
simple fact: Everything has a beginning.

Nothing always existed. Everything had an Innovator.

We all know who invented telephones and lightbulbs, but the humbler innovations are made anonymously. But there was a first paper airplane, a first pair of jeans cut off into shorts, a first paper-clip necklace. And traveling back in time: a first back scratcher, a first birthday present, a first hole designated as the one to throw garbage in.

Once a good idea spreads, however, it's hard to believe it didn't always exist.

Take detective stories. The first was written by Edgar Allan Poe in 1841. (Spoiler alert: The monkey did it.) Over the next 163 years Poe's innovation infected countless books, films, plays, and TV shows. And like most rampant viruses, the detective character has mutated into every imaginable form: little old ladies who solve crimes, medieval monks who solve crimes, cats who solve crimes, even criminals who solve crimes.

My dad used to devour mystery novels (about epidemiologists who solve crimes, I'm sure) until one day he read an interview with a real homicide detective in Los Angeles. The guy had been on the force for over forty years, and in all that time not a single major crime had ever been solved by an amateur detective.

Not one.

With that in mind, we took Mandy's phone to the cops.

"Relationship to the missing person?"

"Uh, co-worker? I mean, she gets me jobs."

"And where do you work, Hunter?"

"Nowhere in particular. I'm a . . . consultant. A shoe consultant. Mostly shoes."

Detective Machal Johnson looked me up and down.

"Shoe consultant? Good money in that?"

"I mostly get paid in shoes."

One eyebrow was slowly rising. "Okay. Shoe consultant." The detective typed as he talked: sleepily. I could have input the letters faster into my cell phone (if I'd had one). Johnson's ancient computer looked equally slow. The screen was all one greenish color—the glowing letters fireflies trapped in mint toothpaste. "So this Mandy Jenkins is also a . . . shoe consultant?"

"Yeah, I guess that's what you'd call her."

"And when do you guess you last saw her?"

"Yesterday, about five."

"Less than twenty-four hours ago?"

Jen nudged me, and Detective Johnson looked like he was about to take his hands off the keyboard, but I didn't let him. It had taken us an hour to get to this point, past desk sergeants, metal detectors, and a wide variety of unimpressed expressions.

"She was supposed to meet us this morning," I said. "At Lispenard and Church."

He sighed and typed, mouthing the street names. "Any evidence of foul play?"

"Yes. We found her phone." I placed it on the detective's desk.

He turned it over once in his hand. "That's all? No purse? No wallet?"

"That's it."

"Where?"

"Where we were supposed to meet her. It was just inside this abandoned building."

He put the phone down. "You were supposed to meet her inside an abandoned building?"

"No, on the corner. But the phone was inside, nearby. And there's a picture on it."

"A picture on the building?"

"No, on the phone. It's also a camera. That's the picture on the screen."

Putting on half-lens glasses that seemed to suddenly age him, the detective peered at the phone. "Huh. What do you know." He took in the tiny lens next to the antenna, squinted at the screen, and gave it a New York cop's version of the Nod. "And what exactly is that a picture of?"

"A face in the dark. We saw that guy."

"What guy?"

"The guy in the picture."

"There's a guy in the picture?"

"You have to use wax paper to see it."

"He chased us," Jen said.

Detective Johnson looked at her, then his eyes swept back and forth across the space between us a few times, an alien watching a tennis match and trying to grasp the rules. "Have you tried calling your friend?"

"We can't. That's her phone."

"At her office? At her home?"

"Sure, her roommate too. But we just got machines."

"Okay." Detective Johnson pushed his glasses up higher onto his nose and settled back from the rigors of typing into the creaky comfort of his office chair. "I know you're concerned about your friend, but let me tell you this about missing people: Ninety-nine out of hundred aren't missing. They had a personal emergency, or got stuck on a train, or went out of town and forgot to tell you. With adults we don't even start looking for twenty-four hours unless there's a reason to believe foul play was involved."

I felt Jen twitching next to me. She was dying to get out of the cop shop, back to her new job as an Innovator who solves crimes.

"Now, you did find her phone, which you are *sure* is hers . . ." (I nodded like a puppy) ". . . but that's not really a sign of foul play. Until she's been missing for twenty-four hours, it's just a lost phone. At which point you should have her roommate or a relative or some other adult call me if she's still missing. I'll keep your information on file."

I could tell from his tone it was useless arguing. "Oh. Thanks."

"So, do you want to turn in this phone as lost property, or would you like to save your friend some paperwork when she reappears and hold on to it?" He held out the phone, making it clear who was being saved from paperwork.

"Sure," Jen said eagerly. "We can give it to her. No trouble."

Detective Machal Johnson nodded slowly, ceremoniously handing the phone back to me.

"Your public-spiritedness is appreciated, I assure you."

ELEVEN

OUTSIDE THE COP SHOP:

"What now?"

"There's only one place to go. Back."

"Crap."

We approached the abandoned building cautiously, coming up Lispenard, urban commandos dodging from cover to cover—mounds of trash bags buzzing with midday flies, the half concealment of a phone booth, crouching behind doorways and stoops.

Actually, it was fun.

Until we spotted them.

The plywood doors were wide open, the padlock swinging on its chain. A rental truck sat blocking half the street, its elevator ascending with a whine, stacked high with boxes of the shoes.

"They're moving," Jen said.

We were hidden behind a steel-clad loading dock that thrust into the street, hot under our fingertips from the noon sun. We spoke in short bursts, as if on radios.

"Bald guy, by the door," I said.

"I count two more."

"Roger that."

"Roger what?"

"What?"

SoHo tourists walked by, casting puzzled looks in our directions. Hadn't they ever seen a stakeout before?

Our bald friend watched the work with a foreman's lazy disinterest while a woman stacked boxes on the curb. She was arrayed in a style commonly known as Future Sarcastic: a T-shirt emblazoned with a big-eyed alien, flight-suit trousers with dozens of gadget-shaped pockets, silver hair shining in the sun. Everything but the jet pack.

The guy riding the truck's elevator was muscular and lean, very dark. He was wearing a trucker cap and cowboy boots, jeans and a mesh shirt that showed off his muscles. In a friendlier context I would have pegged him as a gay bodybuilder doing an ironic take on NASCAR fandom. But alongside the other two, he looked more like one of many hopefuls sent down by central casting to try out for the part of Thug #3 in a hip new thriller.

Of which we were the unlikely heroes, I reminded myself.

"What do we do?" I asked, trying not to catch the eye of a curious young mother pushing a double-wide stroller past our position.

Jen pulled out her cell phone, starting thumbing. "Well, I'm inputting the license number of that truck."

"It's a rental."

"And rental places keep records."

"Oh, yeah." Maybe if I'd read more books about shoe consultants who solved crimes, I would've figured that out myself.

"And you should be taking pictures."

"Good idea. I mean, roger that."

I pulled out Mandy's phone and started to shoot. Between the five-millimeter lens and lack of zoom, they'd be pretty useless pictures, I was sure. But it was better than just standing there and being gawked at by passersby.

"Excuse me, is Broadway and Ninety-eighth Street around here?"

I looked up from my crouch at the two girls in their Jersey glitter shirts and floppy shoes, white capri pants tied at the calf with drawstrings, so last summer. I had to take pity on them—plus they were giving away our position.

"Yeah, it's about two blocks east"—hooking my thumb over my shoulder—"and about a hundred and ten blocks north."

"A hundred and ten blocks? That's far, right?"

I told them where to catch the 1 train.

"Your public-spiritedness is appreciated, I assure you," Jen drawled after the two had left, uncertainly repeating my directions to each other as they passed out of earshot.

"After when are you not supposed to wear white pants?" I asked.

"Roughly 1979."

I pointed. "They're leaving."

The truck was loaded, the bald guy scraping shut the building's doors. The shoes were going away. I thought of rising and dashing after the truck, jumping on just as it exceeded running speed, concealing myself behind boxes until I reached their evil lair, sneaking out and stealing a henchman's uniform, and, after a few captures and escapes, pulling the levers that made the whole place explode. And I realized why no crimes were ever solved by amateurs.

"There's nothing we can do, right?"

"Nope," said Jen as the truck pulled away.

The ground floor was empty.

"This sucks," I said.

We'd squeezed our way in through the wooden doors, which the bald guy hadn't bothered to chain together very tightly. There was no point. Every last box was gone.

I checked Mandy's phone for the time. It was coming up on two o'clock, only two and a half hours since we'd been here.

Jen surveyed the empty cavern of the building, her eyes scanning the floor inch by inch, finding nothing but spotless concrete.

"We should have come back earlier," Jen said quietly. "The shoes were right *here*."

"Did you forget the running-for-our-lives thing?"

"Overrated." Jen sighed. "There must be something we missed before."

She wandered off again, leaving me in the shaft of light by the doors, where I silently listed the reasons amateurs didn't solve crimes in the real world. Professional detectives would have sealed off the building with yellow tape from the start, dusting for fingerprints, searching for records of ownership and work permits. Actual police would have arrested the big guy in black and intimidated him into talking. Real cops wouldn't have run to the nearest coffee shop and then their friend's house to make expert use of wax paper. (Okay, maybe a coffee shop would have come into play, but they would have sent the rookie for doughnuts, leaving plenty of manpower for stretching out the yellow tape.) Non-amateurs might have the first clue how to take the license number of a rental truck and turn it into an address. I sure didn't.

And most importantly, a genuine crime solver wouldn't be terrified by the idea that the bad guys had his cell phone and were trying to find him. Real police were machines for turning coffee into solved crimes. I was a machine for turning coffee into jangled nerves.

"Hunter?" Jen's voice came out of the gloom, jangling my nerves.

"What?"

"Looks like someone left you a message."

She emerged, squinting and holding an envelope. A gray square of duct tape curled from it, the envelope glowing white in the gloom, carrying the letters *H-U-N-T-E-R* in red marker.

Her green eyes were wide, pupils huge in the dim light. "This was taped to the wall back there. Right where the shoes were."

I swallowed, holding out my hand. I'd seen Mandy scrawling notes during focus groups, her handwriting slanted, impatient, and unreadable. But my name stretched across the envelope in controlled and implacable letters.

"Aren't you going to open it?"

I took a slow breath and tore gingerly at the paper, not sure what I was nervous about. A letter bomb? Contact poison? The ace of spades?

It was two tickets.

I stared at them dumbly until Jen pulled one from my hand and read aloud.

"'You are invited to the launch party of *Hoi Aristoi,* the magazine for those with discriminating incomes.' Huh. It's tonight."

I cleared my throat. "That isn't Mandy's handwriting."

"Didn't think so."

"They know my name."

"Of course they do. They called a friend of yours, who saw the ID and answered, 'Hi, Hunter.' And the next number they call, they say, 'Hey, I'm a friend of Hunter's,' and maybe ask for your home number, and so on."

I nodded. Piece by piece, my identity would be sucked out of the phone. Those Finns had done such a terribly good design job, making it the center of my life, filled with my friends' names and numbers, my favorite MP3s, pictures of my sock drawer.

I handed the tickets back. "So what are these about?"

"Search me. Have you ever heard of *Hoi Aristoi?*"

A vague memory of prelaunch buzz trickled into my mind. "I think it's the latest magazine for trendies with too much money. A waste of trees. I think that Hillary Winston-hyphen-Smith did PR for them."

Jen plucked one from my hand, turned it over, and nodded.

"I guess they're exactly what they say they are."

"Which is?"

"An invitation. And I suppose we should go."

TWELVE

"GO?"

"We've got to, Hunter."

I stared at Jen in bewilderment.

"Look, they already know your name; they could probably find out a lot more if they tried."

"Gee, that makes me feel better."

"But these tickets show they haven't yet. Because what they really want to know is how far *you're* willing to go to find *them*."

"What are you talking about?"

Jen pulled me deeper into the empty building, pointing to a spot my unadjusted eyes couldn't see.

"They left the envelope there, right where the boxes were. They knew that if you really gave a damn about all this, you'd come back here, looking for Mandy and the shoes. So they left you a message: 'Want to know more? Show up tonight.'"

"And save them the trouble of finding me."

She nodded. "Very clever of them. Because it's the best way to find out who they are."

"It's the best way to wind up missing, like Mandy."

Jen crossed her arms, staring at the blank expanse of wall. "True, which would suck. So we have to do this in some way they don't expect."

"How about not at all? They won't expect that, I bet."

"Or maybe . . ." Jen turned and touched my hair, pulling a strand of my longer right-side bangs aside. She touched my cheek, and I felt my own heartbeat there beneath her fingertips.

"That guy only saw you for a few seconds," she said. "Do you think he'd recognize you if he saw you again?"

I tried to ignore what Jen's touch was doing to me. "Yes. Didn't we just learn that human beings are machines for turning coffee into facial recognition?"

"Yeah, but it was pretty dark in here."

"He also saw us upstairs in the sunlight."

"But it was blinding up there, and you didn't have your new haircut."

"My new *what?*"

"And the party invite says, 'Dress for success—black tie preferred.' I bet you look completely different in a tuxedo."

"I bet I look completely different with my face caved in."

"Come on, Hunter. Don't you want a makeover?"

Jen's fingers moved to my jaw, gently turning my head so that she could see my profile. Her gaze lingered, so intent I could almost feel it. I turned and looked into her eyes, and something sparked between us in the darkness.

"I think shorter and blond," she said, holding my gaze. "I do a mean dye job, you know."

I nodded slowly, so that her fingertips brushed along my cheek. She dropped her hand and looked up at my bangs again. Like any serious Logo Exile, Jen no doubt cut and colored her own hair. I imagined her fingers massaging my wet scalp and knew the argument was over.

"Well," I said, "if they want to, they'll find me sooner or later anyway."

Jen smiled. "Might as well look sharp when they do."

◇　◆　◇

"What would you usually wear to a formal party?"

"Formal? Anything without a tie. I've got this Nehru collar shirt. That and a black jacket, I guess."

"Right, sounds very you. So for the non-you we'll go for a bow tie."

"A what?"

"They're over here, I think."

We were in a certain well-known store associated with Thanksgiving Day parades and Santa Claus movies. It was not a place Jen or I usually shopped. But that was the point, I was learning. We were shopping for the non-Hunter.

The non-Hunter wore bow ties. He preferred crisply laundered white shirts and tasteful silk vests. The non-Hunter seemed not to know it was summer outside; I suppose he went from one air-conditioned place to another in an air-conditioned limousine. He was going to blend right in at a party for *Hoi Aristoi*.

And hopefully, the non-Hunter would fly in the face of all the evidence one might collect from the real Hunter's cell phone. To pursue the anti-client, I would become the anti-me.

The real me checked out a random price tag. "These jackets are like a thousand bucks!"

"Yeah, but we can return everything Monday and get a refund. Fashion shoots do it all the time. You've got a credit card, right?"

"Uh, yeah." The refund plan seemed like a risky proposition to me, but Innovators generally lack the risk-assessment gene. Jen wandered the aisles in a kind of trance, her fingers trailing in the textures of overpriced fabrics, sucking up the ambience of this entirely different set of New York tribal costumes.

She stopped to spin a rack of cripplingly expensive bow ties, and my nerves blipped her radar. "Relax, Hunter. We've got four hours before the party officially starts. Which means five before anyone will show. All day to get you dressed."

"What about getting *you* dressed, Jen?"

She nodded, sighing. "I've been giving that some thought. It'll be too easy to recognize us if we're together. So I'll probably look for some alternate mode of disguise."

"Wait. We're not going together?"

"Hey, this isn't too bad."

She pulled out a jacket, a jet black synthetic that sucked the light from the room, double-breasted and textured like rough and supple paper.

"Wow, cool."

"Yeah, you're right. Too you." She put it back. "We need something that doesn't make a statement. Something that's not trying very hard."

"What? You think I'm trying too hard?"

Jen laughed, turning from the racks to catch my eye. "Just hard enough."

She spun away and headed off toward more jackets, leaving me to contemplate these words. I wound up hanging out in front of a triple mirror, wallowing in the discomfort of seeing what I looked like from unfamiliar directions. Did my ears really stick out like that? Surely that was not my profile. And when had my shirt gotten half tucked in at the back?

Then I noticed what I was wearing. When cool hunting, I usually disappear into corduroys, sportswear, and laundry-day splendor, turning invisible. But this morning I'd unconsciously slipped into my real clothes. Generic corduroy had resolved into baggy black painters, the usual oversized chewing-gum-colored tee replaced by a light gray wife beater under an open black shirt with a collar. No wonder my parents had noticed, somehow reading the signs, resulting in the unexpected psychic leap when Mom had asked whether I liked Jen.

Maybe it was obvious to everyone. Maybe I was trying too hard.

"I think we're all set." Jen appeared behind me, the mirrors splitting her into multiple views, full hangers swinging from one hand. I took them from her, regressing to when Mom used to take me shopping, and equally unsure of the result.

"Are you sure we couldn't just disguise ourselves as waiters or something?"

"Yeah, right. That is so *Mission Impossible.*" (By which she meant the original TV show and not the movie franchise, so I'll allow it.)

She reached up to ruffle my hair, checking out the angles in the mirror, and smiled. "Take one last look, Hunter. By tonight you won't recognize yourself."

THIRTEEN

"THIS IS GOING TO STING," JEN SAID.

It did. Of course it did.

Bleach is acid, the great destroyer. You see, each of your hairs is protected by an outer layer called a cuticle, which holds in the pigment that gives the hair its color. The purpose of bleach is to destroy these cuticles so that all the pigment falls out. It's quick and dirty. Like smashing a bunch of fish tanks to release the fish, it leaves a mess. That's why if you go on to add coloring, a little bit swims down the drain every time you take a shower. Your fish tanks are broken.

I had known all this, but only in theory, because I'd always dyed my hair blacker, not lighter. (I was just adding more fish, not getting rid of the old ones.) So when Jen started daubing toothpaste-consistency acid into my hair, I wasn't prepared.

"That stings!"

"That's what I said."

"Yeah, but . . . *ow.*"

It felt like many thousands of mosquitoes were visiting my scalp. Like a bald man who'd fallen asleep at the beach. Like my hair was on fire.

"How's that?"

"A lot like . . . having acid on my head."

"Sorry, but I maxed out the solution strength. We're going for major transformation here. It won't hurt as much next time, you know."

"*Next* time?"

"Yeah. Your scalp loses a lot of feeling after the first bleach job."

"Great," I said. "I was looking to get rid of some of those extra scalp nerves."

"No pain, no gain."

"I'm feeling the gain."

She covered my head with a piece of aluminum foil—saying helpfully, "This makes it hotter, to strengthen the chemical reaction"—then flipped another chair out and sat down across from me.

We were in Jen's kitchen, which was small but clearly the workplace of a committed cook. Pots and pans hung from the ceiling, clanking lightly in the breeze from an exhaust fan working to remove the smell of hair acid. Two thousand dollars' worth of recently purchased non-Hunter party-wear hung among the pans, still covered in plastic to make sure my next credit card bill wouldn't kill me.

Jen lived here with her older sister, who was trying to break into being a dessert chef. Many of the blackened iron pans suggested the shapes of macaroons and ladyfingers, and there was a series of sifts for refining flour down to invisible dust.

The kitchen was retro or maybe just old. The chair on which I quietly writhed was vintage chrome and vinyl, matching the table's green-and-gold-speckled Formica. The refrigerator was also 1960s era, with a stainless-steel door handle shaped like a giant trigger.

As the acid slowly flayed my scalp, I found myself desperate for distraction.

"Has your sister had this place long?"

"It was my parents' when they first moved in together. We lived here until I was twelve, but they kept it after the Day of Darkness."

"The Day of Darkness?"

"When we moved out to Jersey."

I tried to imagine a whole family living here, and my melting-scalp discomfort was tinged with claustrophobia. Off the kitchen were two other smallish rooms with air-shaft windows. That was the whole place.

"Four people in this place? New Jersey must have looked pretty good."

Jen made a gagging noise. "Oh, sure. Great for my parents. But everyone out there thought I was a *freak,* with my kiddie-punk purple streaks and homemade clothes."

I thought about my own big move. "Well, at least you weren't too far away from home to visit."

She sighed. "Might as well have been. By the time I was fourteen, my Manhattan friends had all dumped me. Like I'd turned into a Jersey girl or something."

"Ouch."

I remembered my peek into Jen's room when we'd arrived. It was classic Innovator: furniture collected off the street, a shelf overrun with notebooks, a dozen half-completed projects in paper and cloth. Three walls were covered, one by magazine clippings, one by a collage of found photographs she'd picked up off the street, and the last by a bulletin board painted to resemble a basketball court, on which magnetic *X*s and *O*s held up pictures of players male and female. The loft bed made a cave for a small desk, where a laptop flickered in invisible communion with a wireless hub hanging on the wall. All the frantic clutter of a cool girl trying to make up for the Lost Years.

"When did you move back?"

"Last year, as soon as they let me. But it's hard to get your cool back after you lose it, you know? It's like when you're walking down the street, perfectly dressed, grooving to some excellent sound track in your head, and you trip on a crack in the sidewalk? A second ago you were so cool, and suddenly . . . everyone's just looking at you. You're back in Jersey." She shook her head. "Is that hurting?"

"How could you tell?"

"Something about the grinding teeth."

"When does it stop?"

She weighed invisible objects in her hands. "Depends. We can stop it anytime. But for every second of pain now, you'll be blonder and less Hunter-like when you come face-to-face with the bad guys tonight."

"So, it's pain now or pain later."

"Pretty much." She pulled the fridge's giant trigger and reached in for a carton of milk. From the jangling metal overhead, she acquired a mixing bowl and poured some in. "This is ready for when you can't stand it anymore."

"Milk?"

"It neutralizes the bleach. It's like your head has an ulcer."

"That feels accurate." I steeled myself, eyes on the undulating white surface of the milk settling in the bowl. Blonder was better, safer. But the route to blond was long and hot.

"Distract me more," I pleaded.

"You grew up in the city?"

"No. Moved here from Minnesota when I was thirteen."

"Huh, the opposite of me. What was that like?"

I chewed my lip. It wasn't an experience I talked about much, but I had to talk about something. "Eye-opening."

"What do you mean?"

A finger of acid was making its way down the back of my neck. I rubbed it.

"Come on, Hunter, you can make it. Become one with the bleach."

"I *am* becoming one with the bleach!"

She laughed. "Just talk to me, then."

"Okay, here's the thing: Back in Fort Snelling, I was pretty popular. Good at sports, lots of friends, teachers liked me. I thought I was cool. But my first day in New York, I turned out to be the least cool kid in school. I dressed from a mall, listened to total MOR, and didn't have the first clue that people in other places did anything else."

"Ouch."

"No, this is ouch. That was more like . . . being suddenly erased."

"That doesn't sound like much fun."

"Not really." My voice cracked a bit, related to the acid on my head. "But once I realized I wasn't going to have any friends, the pressure was off, you know?"

She sighed. "I do know."

"So it got kind of interesting. Back in Minnesota we had maybe four basic cliques: ropers, jocks, freaks, and socials. But suddenly I was in this school with eighty-seven different tribes. I realized that there was this massive communication system all around me, a billion coded messages being sent every day with clothes, hair, music, slang. I started watching, trying to break the code."

I blinked and took a breath. My head was melting.

"Go on."

I tried to shrug, which reorganized the pain in new and interesting ways. "After a year of watching, I went on to high school, where I got to reinvent myself."

She was silent for a moment. I hadn't meant to get into quite so much detail and wondered if the acid was seeping into my brain, making it porous.

"Wow." She took one of my hands. "Sounds horrible."

"Yeah, it sucked."

"But that's how you got into cool hunting, isn't it?"

I nodded, which sent a second little trail of acid down my back. My scalp was sweating now, trickles slow and incendiary, like flowing lava, as seen on a certain cable channel associated with wildlife, experimental aircraft, and volcanoes. I forced my mind away from the image.

"I started taking pictures on the street, trying to figure out what was cool and what wasn't and why. I got a little obsessive, which happens sometimes, and started writing commentary. Then that turned into a blog. And about three years ago Mandy saw my site and sent me an e-mail: 'The client needs you.'"

"Huh. Happy ending."

I tried to agree, but at that moment the only happy ending would have been my head in a bucket of milk. A bathtub of milk. A swimming pool of ice cream.

"I guess that's why your bangs are so long," Jen said.

"What?"

"I've been wondering about your hair. It seemed kind of weird that you were this cool hunter, but you had those bangs hiding your face." She reached across and flicked away a trickle of lava from my forehead just before it dribbled into my left eye. "But now I get it. When you moved here from Minnesota, you lost all your confidence. You had to hide for a while. So it makes sense: You're still hiding some of yourself."

I cleared my throat. "You think my bangs lack confidence?"

"I think maybe you're still scared that you might lose your cool again."

I felt my face flush. The kitchen felt hot and small and crowded. I couldn't tell how much was annoyance, how much was embarrassment, and how much was the acid on my head. I wanted to reach up and tear my scalp off, to scratch the giant mosquito bite that was my brain. The bleach was definitely leaking through.

Jen smiled and leaned forward until her face was inches away. She pursed her lips, and I thought for a crazy second that she was going to kiss me. My anger dissolved into surprise.

But instead she blew lightly, a delicate wind that cooled my damp face, sending a shudder through me.

"Don't worry," she said softly. "I'm going to fix all that. Those bangs are doomed."

I couldn't stay that close, so I laughed and turned away.

She waited until I turned back. "I know how it feels, Hunter. I lost my cool too."

"Not really, though. They just didn't get you."

"No, really. No matter what I did over there, I couldn't crack the code. All those girls in my eighth-grade class probably still think I'm some loser who writes poetry."

"Oh! Body blow," I said, trying to smile. But the memory of my first year in the city wasn't done with me yet. It was always there, a cold lump of clay in my stomach. I remembered the lump growing heavier every step of the way to school. Recalling that awful loneliness had invited it into me again, as if it belonged inside me.

I took a breath and willed myself into the present, where I was cool. Well, burning up actually and hunted by implacable foes and without my cell phone. But *cool,* right?

"I always thought aluminum foil on your head was supposed to prevent mind reading," I said.

Jen grinned, but only for a moment. "It's not mind reading. Like you said, it's all about reading codes. I just read a different set than you."

"You mean you use your powers for good?"

"Instead of helping giant shoe corporations? Maybe." She stood and dropped a washcloth into the mixing bowl of milk and lifted it, dripping, into the air before my wide eyes. She carried it behind me. "See what you think of my powers after *this.*"

I felt the aluminum foil whisked away, and a cool and sovereign mass descended upon my head, transforming the burning acid into something benign, finally ending my agony.

"Oh . . . ," I groaned.

There were still a few trickles of acid coursing down my neck and flickers of annoyance from being read like a book. It was much better when I was the one reading the codes. Everybody hates old pictures of themselves.

But when I looked in the bathroom mirror, I liked the result.

No pain, no gain.

FOURTEEN

I OPENED THE DOOR TO MY PARENTS' APARTMENT NERVOUSLY.

How was I nervous? Let me count the ways. There was the two thousand dollars' worth of clothing on the hangers in my hand—one false move and I wouldn't be getting a refund. There was the mysterious anti-client pursuing me, who might already have this address. And there was my head, which was an entirely new color. Every reflective surface between Jen's apartment and mine had brought me up short. The peroxide stranger stared back at me all the way home, as perplexed as I was by the situation.

"Hello?" I called.

And of course there were my parents, who were going to freak when they saw my hair cropped and dyed. Not that they'd mind—they might even like it—but they were going to ask a lot of questions. And when they found out that Jen-the-new-girl had done it . . .

I shuddered.

"Hello?"

No answer. No sounds except passing sirens, water running through the pipes, and the ambient buzz of the neighbors' air-conditioning. I closed the door, deciding I was probably safe. My parents' apartment building is more than a century old. Made of stone, it's cool even in summer and always feels secure.

Besides, there's a reason why slasher movies are always set in suburbia or out in the country. New York City dwellings have hardwood doors with metal jackets and dead-bolt locks and bars on the window. You pretty much notice if someone has broken in. Checking under the bed is not required.

I checked the time. It was two hours before I was supposed to arrive at the party. Jen was showing up earlier, separately, to help maintain our anonymity. She hadn't even told me what her disguise was going to be. I had a feeling she didn't know yet.

I hung the clothes in my room, then went to the bathroom and took another long look at myself, watching in amazement as the peroxide stranger mirrored every movement.

As I said, most Logo Exiles cut their own hair, but that's not a skill that always translates to cutting someone else's. Jen had done a good job on me, though. The cut was short and severe, and the acid had left my hair almost white. My still-black eyebrows stood out in lone contrast against my skin, exaggerating every expression. I looked a little like a gangster in a too-hip French movie, but definitely a self-assured one. Maybe Jen was right, and I had been hiding behind my bangs.

Strange. With my entire face at long last showing, I was in disguise, marveling at the sense of dislocation as I played mirror mime with the peroxide stranger. If *I* didn't recognize me, why should anyone else?

One shower later, I got dressed.

In the interest of actually getting my two-thousand-dollar refund, I decided to leave the tags on the clothes. This was to prove a painful mistake, but at first I hardly noticed the tiny plastic twigs. Everything fit perfectly, with the sumptuous well madeness of expensive clothing. The black pants were classically pleated, the gleaming white tuxedo shirt battened down with onyx cuff links. Argyle-patterned suspenders defined my shoulders. It all slid on so easily, each garment transforming me a little more into the non-Hunter, increasing my confidence that I would be unrecognizable tonight. Not to mention my confidence that I looked pretty damn good.

Until I reached the confidence-shattering bow tie. Which, of course, I didn't have the first idea how to tie.

The bulbous little flap of black and shiny cloth drooped lifelessly around my neck, offering no clues as to how it might work. I was long on historical knowledge about neckwear but very short on the practical. Bow ties just weren't a part of my world of baggy pants and T-shirts, skater labels and the latest cross-trainer. When it came to bow ties, I was still from Minnesota.

Looking at the clock, I discovered that I had thirty minutes to reverse-engineer five hundred years of necktie technology.

Not for the first time, I cursed the Little Ice Age. . . .

The next time you're forced to wind a tie around your neck, blame the sun.

As any corporate drone or private-school kid knows, ties are basically uniforms—most of us wear them because we have to, not because we want to. Not surprisingly, the earliest-known neckwear is found on men who didn't have a choice, Chinese soldiers in about 250 BC. Roman soldiers started wearing ties about four centuries later. (Apparently noodles weren't the only thing the Italians had delivered from the Chinese.) History teaches us that people who wore ties were all pretty much forced to—until about five hundred years ago.

Then it got cold everywhere.

The sun began to sputter, putting out less and less heat. Slowly but surely the Little Ice Age arrived, with serious consequences. Glaciers ate towns in France, an ice-skating craze swept Holland, and all the Vikings in Greenland died. That's right, *Vikings* didn't make it through the winters. That's pretty cold.

And everyone started wearing scarves, indoors and out.

At some point, of course, some Innovator became bored with this ice-age dress code and started playing with his scarf, making it thinner and easier to tie and coming up with new ways to tie it. The craze caught on, giving people something to do during those long winters, I guess. Neckwear exploded. The cravat, the stock, and the Steenkirk were all invented, to be tied in complicated knots called the "philosophical," the nineteenth century, *Neckclothitania,* lists seventy-two ways to tie a tie. Talk about mathematical.

Fortunately for you and me, the sun came back, and things got warmer and simpler.

Nowadays some lucky men manage to wear ties only for weddings, funerals, and job interviews. The last knots standing are the Windsor, the half Windsor, and the four-in-hand. And only three varieties of neckwear remain: the bow tie, string ties for cowboys, and the regular kind. And with global warming ratcheting up the heat, it may only be a matter of time before we get rid of those.

Until that fine day comes, however, there's always the information desk of the New York Public Library.

"Hello? I need to know how to tie a bow tie."

"Yes, we have books on etiquette and grooming."

"Actually, I don't have time for a book. I need to know now." I checked the kitchen clock. "I have to be out the door in twenty-six minutes."

"Uh, hold, please."

While she went to get a copy of *Neckclothitania* or, I hoped, *Bow Ties for Dummies,* I pulled the landline phone to the bathroom mirror. Mandy's cell phone would have been easier, but it didn't feel right to use up her minutes. The squiggly landline cord stretched the distance reluctantly, shivering with the quiet fury of massive potential energy. If it slipped from my grasp, it was going to shoot back into the kitchen at a speed that would shatter linoleum.

I secured it carefully between neck and shoulder, preparing to do battle.

Don't try this at home.

"Okay, sir. Post or Vanderbilt?"

"Excuse me?"

"Emily Post's book of etiquette or Amy Vanderbilt's?"

"Post, I guess."

"Okay, the first thing to remember is that it's just like tying your shoes."

"But around your neck."

"Right. First, the tie should be hanging loose, one end longer than the other. From now on I will refer to this as 'the long end.'"

"Done." This wasn't so hard.

"Now cross the long end over the short end, then pass it back and up through the loop. Tighten the knot loosely around your neck. It'll be much easier if you imagine you're tying a shoe."

"Uh . . ." The awesome complexity of Jen's rising-sun laces swam before my eyes. I banished all thoughts of shoes from my mind. "Okay, done."

"Now fold the lower hanging end up and to the left. Make sure the unfolded end is hanging down over the front of the bow. Okay?"

"Er, yes."

"Now form an angle loop with the short end of the tie, which should be crossing left. Then drop the long end that's up by your neck over this horizontal loop. Still with me?"

"Nnnyes."

"Now place right forefinger, pointing up, on bottom half of hanging part. Pull the bow ends forward and gently squeeze them together, forming an opening behind them."

"Erf?"

"Now pass up behind the front loop and poke the resulting loop through knot behind the front loop."

"Wait, how many loops are there now?"

She paused, presumably to count. "Two, plus the one around your neck. You should be ready to tighten the knot by adjusting the ends of both of them."

"I think it's—"

"Emily says, 'Remember to express your individuality. It shouldn't be too perfect.'"

"Oh, I wish you'd told me that earlier. We may have to start over."

"Well, maybe perfect is okay."

"Not this kind of perfect."

"All right." Rustle of pages. "First, the bow tie should be hanging loose around your neck, one end longer than the other. From now on I will refer to this as 'the long end. . . .'"

And so on, for the most arduous seventeen minutes of my life, which from now on I will refer to as "bow tie hell." Eventually, however, and mostly of its own volition, the bow tie became tied, displaying a degree of imperfection that exaggerated my individuality only slightly.

I was ready to go, but in my post-bow-tie exhaustion, I realized that I hadn't eaten since breakfast. Whether or not the anti-client would see through my disguise and kidnap me tonight, I wouldn't make it very far without blood sugar.

In the kitchen my hand paused a few inches from the refrigerator door. Atop the fridge the message light on my parents' answering machine was blinking. I swore at myself for not having checked earlier. Normally no one ever called me on the landline, but with my cell phone missing in action, someone might have tried the parental number.

When I pushed the button, my mom's voice declaimed this chirpy, chilling message:

"I hope you check this, Hunter. Good news: Some guy called me and said he found your phone. I didn't know you'd lost it. Anyway, he was really nice. He said he was going to be up in Midtown this afternoon, so he's dropping it by my office. See you tonight."

Beep.

I grabbed the phone and dialed her office, one of the few numbers I knew by heart. Her assistant answered.

"She's already left."

"Did a man come by, a strange man, to leave something?"

He laughed. "Relax, Hunter, he showed up. Really nice guy. Your mother's got your phone and she's bringing it home. I swear—you kids and your phones."

"When did he come by?"

"Uh, right after lunch?"

"And she's okay? She didn't go anywhere with him, did she?"

"Sure, she's okay. Go anywhere? What are you talking about?"

"Nothing. It's just that . . ." He must have dropped by the office to get a look at her. Then he would wait outside until she left and headed for home. He'd bump into her, strike up a conversation, get her somewhere alone. Plenty of chances for that. Mom always took the subway home. Or they could have staged a purse snatching to gather more information.

"It's nothing. Thanks." I hung up.

They might already have my mother as well as Mandy. And even if they'd only gone for her purse, they would definitely have this address now, not to mention the—

I heard keys jangling in the door.

FIFTEEN

THE APARTMENT DOOR SWUNG OPEN, AND WE EXCHANGED terrified stares.

I recovered first, given that it was in fact my mom. Not held hostage with a knife to her neck, just Mom.

She, on the other hand, freaked out. She stared at me for a moment, then down at her keys, at the number on the apartment door, and then back at me.

"Hunter . . . ?"

"Hi, Mom."

The bag of groceries hit the floor, slumping to one side as its forgotten contents settled. She took a few steps forward, taking in my two-thousand-dollar black-tie splendor with her mouth wide open.

"Good God, Hunter, is that you? What happened?"

"I decided to go for a new look."

She blinked once in slow motion. "No shit!"

Having induced mom profanity, I had to chuckle.

She took a few more steps, shaking her head, and reached out to touch my platinum hair.

"Don't worry, Mom, it won't break."

"It looks pretty good. Actually, you look *fabulous,* but . . ."

My hand went to the bow tie. Had it already gone squiggly? "But what?"

"You hardly look like . . . you."

Her voice cracked on the last word, and in one awful moment my mother managed to go all the way from profanity to tears. Her eyes glistened, her lips trembled, and she actually sniffed.

I was appalled.

"Mom."

"I'm sorry." She rested one hand on my shoulder, the other covering her eyes. Her shoulders shook.

"What's wrong? What did I . . . ?"

She looked up at me, and I realized she was laughing now, a deep sound that shook her whole body.

"I'm sorry, Hunter, you just look so damn *different.*"

I took a deep, relieved breath. We were back in profanity territory.

"Yeah, I'm going to this party tonight," I explained. "And it's kind of formal, so Jen and I were hanging out and we figured it would be fun to . . . you know, dress up."

"Jen did that to your hair?"

"Uh, yeah."

"Well . . . well." She cleared her throat, just smiling now, though her eyes still glittered. "You look incredible. When did you learn to tie a bow tie?"

"Recently." I looked at the clock. "Sorry, Mom, but I've got to get to the party. It's way uptown."

"Of course." She nodded, the shock finally releasing its hold on her. Then she giggled. "I'm not going to tell your dad, though. Can't wait until tomorrow morning. Oh, hang on, I almost forgot." She reached into her bag. "This really nice guy—"

"Yeah, I know all about the nice guy."

My phone emerged, and I reached for it. The familiar shape slid into my hand, solid and gloriously real. "Thanks for getting it back for me. The nice guy, he didn't ask any weird questions or anything, did he?"

"Uh, no. He just said he found it in Chinatown."

"Was he a bald guy?"

Her eyes narrowed. "No. Why would he be?"

"Or a silver-haired woman with a big alien face right here?"

"Hunter, how exactly did you lose your phone?"

I shrugged, promising myself to explain everything later. "Just dropped it, I guess. Thanks. I'm glad you're okay."

"Of course I'm okay." She smiled, stepping back to take me in again. "I've survived worse things than you dyeing your hair blond."

I didn't tell her that wasn't what I'd meant, just hugged her.

"Have a good time, Hunter," she said as we pulled apart. "And tell Jen that I really, *really* want to meet her."

I smiled. "I will. I want you to meet her too."

The weird thing was, I really did.

The launch party was at the Museum of Natural History.

The Natural is a sprawling Gothic castle settled against Central Park. The immediate neighborhood, full of park views and private grade schools that cost as much as Ivy League universities, is home turf for the *hoi aristoi,* which is Greek for "aristocrats." Us regular folk, we're the hoi polloi.

I took a cab uptown, a relatively small investment to lower the odds of damaging my two-thousand-dollar outfit. The long summer day hadn't completely given up its steamy grip on New York's asphalt; it was way too hot to be standing on a subway platform in black tie. And too weird. Mom thought I looked good, *I* thought I looked good, but cool is all about context. Among the rest of the hoi polloi, I would probably just look like a penguin.

A hungry penguin. What with my brief, perplexing encounter with Mom, I still hadn't managed to get anything to eat. Hopefully the party would have a few platters of aristocratic food circulating.

In the cab I pulled the two phones from my pocket, mine and Mandy's, comparing them to confirm that my own had actually come back to me. But what did that mean? Maybe the really nice guy who'd returned it was exactly that, and no one was after me. Could Detective Johnson have been right about Mandy? Had she simply been called away to care for a sick relative and lost her phone somehow? Of course, for that to be true, the whole chase through the abandoned building would have to have been a misunderstanding. Or a random crazy guy? A hallucination?

Didn't seem likely.

And even these radical theories didn't explain the *Hoi Aristoi* launch party invitations. The anti-client was real and wanted to talk to me. Probably they had ditched my phone for some random passerby to find. They didn't need it anymore because they knew that I couldn't abandon Mandy to her fate (or resist the lure of the shoes) and that I would be at the party tonight.

Fiddling with the phone's buttons, I decided to call Jen.

"You got Jen's phone. Leave a message."

"It's Hunter. I got my old phone back. Some guy, not a bald one, brought it to my mom at work. I don't know what that means. So, uh, see you later, I guess. That's the plan, right? Um, bye."

I settled back into the taxi seat, wishing she'd answered or at least that I'd managed not to leave such a dorky message. I've never been a fan of voice mail, which is basically a big magnifying glass for anything or anyone that makes you nervous. But surely I had no reason to be nervous around Jen. I thought about all the times she had caught my eye that day, had found reasons to touch me, to keep hanging out with me. Not to mention give me a complete makeover. Jen liked me.

But did she *like* me? I rubbed my temples—the big problem with being dazzled by someone (yes, I was dazzled) is that you wind up too dazzled to see if they're dazzled by you in return. Or something like that. Maybe Jen was just fascinated by the hunt for the missing Mandy. Or maybe she thought I had adventures like this every day and was going to be disappointed when it turned out I didn't. And do girls usually bleach the hair of guys they want to hook up with? Probably not, but maybe Jen did. . . .

Added to this mental remix was a certain awareness that my anxiety was probably focused in the wrong direction. If my disguise didn't work tonight, my crush on Jen was going to be the least of my worries: the anti-client might squash more than my ego.

I thought about all those movies where the doubtful guy says, "But we'll be walking straight into a trap!" And the brave guy says, "Yeah, but that's why they won't be expecting us." Which is, of course, complete crap. The whole point of setting a trap is that you expect someone to walk into it, right?

But they were expecting dark-haired Hunter of the Skater Shorts, not blond non-Hunter the Mighty Penguin.

I took a deep breath. I really needed some food.

By this hour the museum was closed to the public, but its hillside of marble stairs was still dotted with tourists. I joined the other party-bound filtering up through the tired and sunburned clots of camera pointers. We swept gratefully into the museum's air-conditioned cool, women in evening gowns and men in black tie. In the lobby a barosaurus skeleton reared up over our heads, eighty feet high, defending its skeletal young from a skeletal T. rex. I remembered coming here as a kid, wondering why all these dinosaur skeletons were bothering to eat each other when there clearly wasn't much meat on any of them.

The crowd was big enough to disappear into, the horde of voices smoothed to a rumble by marble echoes. Among my fellow penguins I felt very much in disguise, blending into the throng as velvet ropes channeled us from the lobby to the Hall of African Mammals.

This was the old part of the museum, dating to the days when conservationists went to other places, shot animals, brought their corpses back, and stuffed them. Which is a *kind* of conservation, I suppose. In the center of the huge hall a family of stuffed elephants tramped along together, massive and clueless. Set into the walls around us were dioramas— zebras, gorillas, and impalas against painted African landscapes, staring out at us with wide glass eyes, looking paralyzed with surprise, as if no one had told them that tuxedos were required.

The crowd was drifting in slow circles, moving clockwise around the elephants. True to Manhattan form, the party was just now kicking into gear two hours late, everyone grabbing their first drinks. The slow circling gave me the chance to scope things out, searching for a disguised Jen and any sign of the anti-client.

I was jumpy. The little plastic twigs of the clothing's tags were starting to poke, and I was still surprised by glimpses of a certain peroxide stranger in the glass that separated me from the Africa veldt. Every girl of Jen's height dragged my eyes after her, but unless she'd opted for plastic surgery, she wasn't any of them. Of course I flinched whenever a bald head popped up in the edges of my vision, half expecting a powerful hand to land on my shoulder and lead me away to some dark corner of the museum. I moved through the party, nervous and hyper-alert, as if the pair of sleeping lions in the corner diorama were still alive.

To calm myself, I did what comes naturally to any cool hunter: I read the crowd.

The demographic of *Hoi Aristoi* was young and wealthy, the sort of people whose job it is to go to this sort of party. You know who they are. Their names are in bold type in gossip pages, presumably to remind them what they did last week. They were here to refine their social skills, readying themselves for the day when their trust funds would blossom into real inheritances, and they would join the boards of museums and orchestras and opera companies and go to more parties. The odd camera flash snapped, gathering fodder for the Sunday Styles section and celeb magazines' back pages. Apparently *Hoi Aristoi* really had aristocratic roots. Any magazine that could occupy the entire Museum of Natural History for a party was backed by people with serious social connections.

I wondered if any of the people here would ever actually read *Hoi Aristoi*. Would it run advice columns for the single scion? Essays on mink coat maintenance? Bargain buys for the bulimic's bathroom?

Not that the articles really mattered. Magazines are just wrapping for ads, and advertisers must have been lining up to fill the pages of *Hoi Aristoi,* ready to flog Hamptons real estate, deals on drug treatment centers and liposuction, a dozen labels I shall not name. And for every true aristocratic reader would come a hundred wannabes, pitiful creatures willing to buy a handbag or wristwatch advertised, hoping the rest of the lifestyle would somehow follow.

Why did this tribe annoy me so much? It's not like I'm against social hierarchies—my job depends on them. Every cool constituency from hardtop basketballers to Detroit DJs organizes itself into aristocrats and hoi polloi, insiders and nonentities. But this crowd was different. Becoming an *aristoi* wasn't a matter of taste, innovation, or style, but of being born into one of a select hundred or so Manhattan families. Which is why aristocrats don't really have Innovators. For their new looks they rely on designers from Paris and Rome, hired help selected by Trendsetters like Hillary Hyphen. The top of the *Hoi Aristoi* cool pyramid—where the Innovators should be—is chopped off, sort of like the one on the back of the one-dollar bill. (Coincidence? Discuss.)

Suddenly my step faltered, my sour mood lifting. A few yards away two rent-a-models were stationed in front of a trio of bedazzled bison. And they were giving out gift bags.

Filthy rich or bomb-throwing anarchist, *everyone* loves gift bags.

I grabbed one, assuring myself that it was just to look for clues about the party's sponsors. Parties in New York are always multi-corporate orgies, a mix of advertising, guest lists, and giveaways. Gift bags are the final repository of all this cross-marketing, with everyone involved throwing in an abundance of free toiletries, magazines, movie tickets, CD singles, chocolates, and minuscule bottles of liquor. The main sponsors (I don't mind naming brands, because you can't buy them in stores, for reasons that will soon become clear) were *Hoi Aristoi* magazine itself, a spiced rum called Noble Savage, and a new shampoo that went by the peculiar name of Poo-Sham. The big prize in the bag was a free digital camera, no bigger than an old-fashioned cigarette lighter, with the Poo-Sham logo plastered all over it.

A free digital camera as a carrier for advertising. I gave this the Nod.

Man cannot live on gift bags alone, though. I consumed the chocolate and looked around for real food.

A tray went past carrying champagne and orange juice. I grabbed a glass of the juice and gulped, only to discover it was spiked with Noble Savage . . . a *lot* of Noble Savage. I managed not to sputter, drank it down for the sugar, and immediately regretted it. An empty-stomach buzz began to take hold of my brain.

The party's edges softened around me, and I started to see imperfections in my fellow penguins' bow ties. All that individuality being expressed, according to Emily Post. Or had I gone with Vanderbilt? I couldn't remember, which seemed like a bad sign.

Perhaps my anxiety didn't have to do with Mandy's disappearance, the potential dangers of the anti-client, the pretensions of the *hoi aristoi,* or even the mysteries of Jen's affections. It wasn't even low blood sugar. It was much simpler than that.

I was alone at a party.

No one likes to feel left out. Like the small herd of stuffed impalas gazing sightlessly across the room toward me, I was a social animal. And here I was standing in a tuxedo, holding a gift bag and an empty glass of orange juice, feeling alone among a bunch of people I didn't know and instinctively didn't like.

Where was Jen? I thought of calling her but didn't really have anything to report yet. It just looked like any other launch party so far.

At this point I would have settled for a glimpse of the bald guy, even NASCAR Man or Future Woman. Hiding or fleeing would be better than standing around alone. Anything to give me a purpose.

Another tray went by, carrying something that looked like food, and I followed it.

The tray led me down a short hall toward the outer-space section of the museum. The planetarium rose up before me, a huge white globe on curved legs, as awe inspiring as an alien spaceship. Yet as so often happens in museums, I was thinking about food. I plowed after the tray, not catching the white-coated caterer until he was mobbed by a small and hungry crowd.

The tray was covered with sushi experiments gone awry, tiny towers of fish eggs and multicolored tentacles, something that nonmetaphorical penguins might eat. Not exactly what I'd been hunting for, but I grabbed a pair of what looked like plain rice balls and stuffed one into my mouth. Something inside it exploded into saltiness and fishiness, a sushi booby trap. I swallowed anyway, then inhaled the second.

My mouth was so full that I couldn't scream when a certain bald-headed man stepped up next to me.

SIXTEEN

"*MRRF,*" I SAID IN ALARM.

He muttered something incoherent, his eyes drifting past me.

I swallowed the rice ball in a solid, choking clump.

He kept muttering, and gradually I realized that he wasn't muttering at me. A thin black headset stretched in front of his mouth, and his eyes had the faraway look of the homeless and the wireless. He was on a hands-free phone, and his gaze went *straight through me.*

With my blond hair and penguin suit, I was invisible.

I turned and took a few steps away, the tight fist of nerves in my mostly empty stomach slowly unclenching, no longer threatening to squeeze the swallowed-whole sushi back up. I continued toward the planetarium, trying to take even steps, until a hanging beach-ball-sized model of Saturn presented itself.

I ducked behind the planet and counted to ten, waiting for his bald head to appear, another five goons behind him wearing headsets and predatory smiles.

But he didn't come, and I dared a glimpse.

He stood in the same spot, still talking on his headset. He was a non-penguin, dressed in the all black of security personnel and surveying the crowd, clearly on the lookout.

For me.

I smiled. Jen's disguise had worked. He hadn't connected the new non-Hunter with the skater kid he'd seen this morning.

Still, walking back past him seemed like pushing my luck. I looked ahead for another section of the party to explore. In front of me the planetarium was admitting a steady stream of partyers into its maw. A sign announced continuous showings of the new TV ad for Poo-Sham. Inside it would be dark, and I could recover my cool in a familiar focus-group-like setting. Watching advertisements was something I was good at.

I took a deep breath and stepped out from behind the hanging planet, striding purposefully toward the planetarium. On the way I snagged a glass of champagne, straightening my cuff links and feeling very secret agent.

Poo Sham turned out to be some pretty trippy shampoo.

The lights dimmed in the planetarium. The chairs tipped back, and my body sank into the rumbling presence of a museum-class speaker system. Stars shimmered to life above our heads, as crystal clear as on some cold night on a high mountain.

Then a rectangle of light appeared, a giant television screen carving itself out from the universe.

The ad began in the usual shampoo-ad way—a model in the shower, lather covering her head. Then she was dressing, her hair dry and bouncing in slow motion, with the best highlights that special effects could produce. (Somewhere, lower-level Lexa types had acted as machines for turning coffee into highlights.)

Then the model's date arrived. Her Poo-Sham hair dazzled him, and he sputtered, "Did you just shake a tower?"

She smiled vacuously, flicking her hair.

Next they were arriving at the theater, and the usher, tongue-tied by the glamorous hair, babbled, "May I sew you to your sheets?"

Our heroine smiled vacuously, flicking her hair.

Then at dinner the still-bedazzled date ordered "lack of ram with keys and parrots."

Guess what? Smacuous viling, hicking of flair.

The ad ended with a close-up on the bottle and a voice-over:

"Poo-Sham—it horrifies your glare!"

The planetarium went dark, the audience buzzing for a moment in Poo-Sham bemusement and giggles. Then some sort of software freak-out seemed to take over the projector. The entire screen flickered rapidly back and forth from deep blue to blinding red, sending a needle of weirdness deep into my brain.

The flashing stopped as suddenly as it had started, and the stars came back, the lights came up, and people were clapping.

I stumbled out of the planetarium, blinking, having completely forgotten the bald guy, the anti-client, everything. The flashing screen had done something to me.

The champagne glass in my hand was empty, so I grabbed another orange juice from a tray. Half-formed thoughts flickered through me, as if somebody had hit the reboot switch for my brain.

This orange juice turned out to be even more spiked than the first one I'd had, but I needed its cold reality in my hand. So I kept drinking, trying to walk off the weirdness left over from the Poo-Sham experience.

Something was bothering the back of my mind, not allowing me to settle. Like everyone, I've watched a lot of TV, seen *lots* of advertisements. I've even been paid to critique them. But something was deeply wrong with the Poo-Sham ad. Not just the flickering screen at the end, but some even bigger affront to my sensibilities.

It hadn't looked *real*.

You know when you're watching a movie, and someone's watching TV in the movie, and it's showing some TV show that doesn't really exist, with some fake talk-show host they just invented for the movie? And it always looks *wrong?* That happens because you and I, like every other American, are partly machines for turning coffee into TV watching. And we're really, really good at it.

Two seconds after switching on a television show, we know whether it's from the late 1980s or last year and whether it's a cop show or a sitcom or a made-for-TV movie, major network or public broadcasting or the dog-walking channel, all this from subtle clues of lighting, camera angles, and the quality of the videotape. Instantly.

You can't get anything past us.

"Roo-Sham isn't peal," I said aloud.

A men's room door caught the corner of my eye, and I pushed my way in. Setting the empty glass on the sink, I rummaged through my gift bag and found the tiny complimentary bottle of Poo-Sham.

I squished a bit onto one finger. It was bright purple but otherwise looked and smelled like shampoo. Running the water, I rubbed it into a lather. It foamed up in a very shampoolike way.

In the mirror a wild-eyed, peroxided stranger who had clearly gone insane stared back at me.

I frowned. Maybe the day's paranoid proceedings had gone to my head, or maybe Jen's hair acid really had leached into my brain. Apparently Poo-Sham was real. They just had a goofy advertising campaign. I sighed and washed my hands.

For five minutes I washed my hands.

But they remained purple.

◇　◆　◇

Poo-Sham was a sham. It was some sort of seriously strong dye. The entire party was a plot to turn rich people purple.

"This doesn't make any sense," I said to the peroxide stranger, drying my still-purple hands. I'd managed to say it right, so possibly the fluorescent lights were bringing me back to reality. But my hands were shaking from hunger, and I could feel the rum and champagne threatening to make my head spin.

Food was required.

I left the gift bag behind in case there were any more booby traps inside it, keeping only the magazine and the free digital camera. The camera was covered with Poo-Sham logos and therefore the most likely candidate for menace, but it was so little and *cute.* I mean, come on. Free digital camera!

My newly purple hands weren't helping the penguin disguise, so I stuffed them into my pockets, trying to look casual, not like a man who had been dyed twice in one day. I was glad no Poo-Sham had gotten into my new hair.

I pulled out my phone and called Jen, getting her message again. For the hundredth time I wondered where she was. I desperately wanted to tell her about the bald man, the fake shampoo, and its fake ad and see if she'd uncovered anything herself.

Mostly I wanted to ask her: Why would the anti-client want to dye people purple?

A tray went by, tiny double-decker salmon sandwiches. I followed it back toward the Hall of African Mammals, wondering how to reach for one without my purple hands attracting attention.

The bald man was where I'd left him, in the passageway between rooms, still chattering on his headset. I straightened my shoulders, trusting my disguise to get me past once more.

But the bottleneck in the hall brought the waiter to a halt, the mob falling on the sandwiches. They were going fast. I bared my teeth, mildly drunk and thoroughly starving, and decided to risk it. I *had* to have food.

I reached out and snatched a sandwich, shoving half of it into my mouth. Like the rice balls, it was too salty, but I clutched it tightly and kept eating, keeping my back to the bald guy.

No one paid me any notice. The backs of my hands weren't as purple as the palms. I decided to try for one more sandwich before leaving the bald guy behind.

Glancing around at the cluster of salmon eaters, I noticed they all had drinks. Words were slurring, and I head a woman lapse into Poo-Shamese:

"This farty has great pood." Her group dissolved into giggles.

People were getting drunk, of course. The salty food was compelling everyone to imbibe. The Noble Savage was everywhere, and now the free cameras were coming out, giggles and flashes popping from every direction.

Between voracious bites I noticed that the Poo-Sham cameras did that stutter thing, blinking rapidly just before the main flash, to shrink your pupil and prevent satanic red-eye. But the sputtering little flickers were even more distracting than usual. They alternated red and blue, just like the flickering screen that had rocked my brain at the end of the Poo-Sham ad. My head started to throb again.

Was the whole party a trap?

No, I had to be imagining it. One more sandwich and I'd be fine.

As I reached out, a familiar smell wafted into my nostrils.

"Mom?" I said softly. It was one of the scents she'd designed.

I turned around, sandwich in purple hand, and came face-to-face with Hillary Winston-hyphen-Smith.

She blinked, looking from my purple hand to my suddenly pale face, recognition gathering with steady inevitability.

"Hunter?" she murmured.

"You've got the gong rye," I said.

SEVENTEEN

"THAT *IS* YOU!" HILLARY SHRIEKED. HER CLUSTER OF FRIENDS
turned toward me, perhaps expecting some minor celebrity or long-lost
cousin of the Winston-hyphen-Smith clan.

"Uh, hi, Hillary," I said mildly, thinking, *Not the name! Not the
name!*

"My God, *Hunter!* You look completely different!"

The bald guy was facing me, only yards away, and here was Hillary
shouting my name.

"Oh, not really that different." *Don't mention the hair!*

"Yeah, right. What did you do to your *hair,* Hunter?"

I could feel the bald guy's eyes on me, adding up my height and
build, the frequently mentioned name (currently number thirty-two in
popularity), and finally the hair. . . .

"You should really dress up more often," Hillary said, her expression
adding one more terrifying thought to all the others going through my
head. the possibility that Hillary Hyphen was undergoing a revelation that
dorky little skater kid Hunter was growing up into a real cutie.

Then she frowned. "But what's with the purple hands? Is that supposed to be retro punk or something?"

There are times when all you can think to say is:

"I have to go now."

I ignored her surprise and walked away, some anti-starvation auto-pilot in my brain stuffing the last of the salmon sandwich into my face. I didn't have to look back as I walked into the Hall of African Mammals, the glassy eyes of dead animals tracking me, knowing me for a marked man.

There was no doubt in my mind: the bald guy was following me.

My phone rang. Still on autopilot, I answered.

"Yeah?"

A deep voice sent a chill through me: "Hi, Hunter. Like the hair."

Weaving through the throng still circling the elephants, I glanced backward. He was close, making his slow, powerful way through the crowd.

"We want to talk to you."

"Uh, call me tomorrow?"

"In person. Tonight."

I decided to go on the offensive, even as I cowered behind a passel of penguins comparing cummerbunds. "Where's Mandy?"

"She's with us now, Hunter." He paused. "Wait a second, I didn't mean that to sound all creepy."

"Well, it did."

I kept moving, bumped into a woman from behind, and waved an apologetic purple hand when she glared at me.

"Sorry," I said, pulling away.

"Sorry for what?" the bald guy's voice said.

"Not *you*." I looked around, trying to find him again.

He had disappeared.

My eyes darted from gazelles to lions to gorillas, trying to spot the guy again, but his bulky frame and bald head had completely vanished.

"Hunter, this isn't about Mandy; it's about the shoes."

I backed up, trying to look in all directions at once. The guy couldn't do anything to me in the middle of the party, but I didn't want him getting any closer. Dressed like a security guard, he could always drag me off, pretending to be throwing an unruly guest out.

"What about the shoes?" I said.

"We're trying to do a deal. But we have to keep it quiet."

Still no sign of him among the swirling mass of penguins. The cold glass of a diorama window pressed against my back. I felt pinned.

"So you want to keep me quiet? That sounds pretty creepy too."

"It's not like that, Hunter. We wanted you here to show you what we're trying to do. This is about more than just shoes."

"I can see that."

A beeping sound screamed in my ear, demanding my attention. I glanced at the phone's screen.

Jen.

"Uh, could you hang on? Call waiting."

"Hunter, don't—"

I switched over. "Jen! I'm so glad—"

"Turn left, walk."

"Where are you?"

"Go! He's closing in."

I went. Through the door and then down a passage lined with photographs of Antarctica. Then I found myself in a hall of huts and costumes, weapons and tools.

"I seem to be in Africa."

"Go all the way through, then take a right and down the stairs."

Could she see me? There wasn't time to ask.

I came to a red velvet rope at the edge of the party. I looked back.

"Jen?" I called out.

Unless she was disguised as a motionless Yoruba shaman, she wasn't in this room. But the bald guy was still in sight, following with measured steps and the annoyed expression of an ignored authority figure.

"Just keep going," Jen said from my phone. "I'm looking at a map. Run."

I ducked under the velvet rope and turned right, dashing through a darkened room full of stuffed birds behind glass. A wide flight of marble steps appeared on my right.

I didn't bother glancing back, knowing the bald guy was right behind me, and plunged down the unlit steps. My hard-soled shoes sent echoes off the marble, pattering like disappointed tongue clicks from every direction.

I would have killed for some sneakers about then. Or clothes without plastic tags sticking into me.

At the bottom of the stairs I whispered, "Where now?"

"Turn right again. Through the monkey skeletons."

I entered a long hall that ran through the entire course of human evolution—from slothlike primates in trees to a slothlike *Homo remote controllus* watching television in his living room—all in about thirty seconds. Among the darkened exhibits I suddenly felt how alone I was (except for the other monkeys) and began to wonder why I'd left the relative safety of the party.

"See any meteorites yet?" Jen asked.

"Meteorites? Hang on."

The next archway opened into a large square room filled with jagged rocks on pedestals.

"Yes," I whispered. "But *why* am I looking at meteorites?"

"I'm trying to get you out of his sight so we can leave without being followed."

"But I was safe! They're not going to do anything while the party's going."

"Parties don't last forever, Hunter."

I looked back through the darkness and thought I heard slow, deliberate footsteps descending the marble stairs.

"Jen, where are you, anyway?"

"Two floors above you, in a gallery overlooking the elephants. You are hiding now, aren't you?"

I looked back through the monkeys but still couldn't see anyone. There'd been no sign of other human beings since I'd come down the stairs.

Still, hidden was better.

Near the center of the room was a meteorite the size of a car. Big enough to crouch behind. I peeked my head out, training an eye on the approach from the hall of monkey skeletons.

"Okay, hidden now."

"You think he followed you?"

"Definitely," I whispered. "But he doesn't seem to be in a huge hurry to find me. Maybe he's calling up reinforcements."

"Perfect. Just stay hidden. I've got a few more things to check out up here now that they're out of the way."

"Uh, hang on, Jen. Are you using me as a *diversion?*"

"You can outrun him, can't you?"

"What is it with you and running?"

"Listen, call me if you need me, Hunter. If you get bored of the meteorites, there're some really cool gems next door. I love this place."

"I'm thrilled."

"But you should probably stay put. The gems room is a dead end."

"You mean the only way out of here is back the way I came?"

"Yeah. So stay hidden. See you later."

I stayed hidden, crouching behind the big hunk of iron from outer space. As always when anxious, I filled my head with useless information, stealing glances away from the yawning doorway to read the little plaques around me.

It turned out that the big meteorite had been brought to New York by Robert Peary, the North Pole guy. It weighed the yawning doorwaya whopping thirty-four tons, which had made traveling with it by ship exciting. On top of almost swamping Peary's vessel, the mass of iron attracted the needle in the ship's compass, so the navigator never quite knew which direction was which.

I could relate to the feeling.

I imagined the bald guy whipping out a compass and following it straight to me.

But strangely, crouching in the darkness calmed my nerves, repairing whatever circuits had been damaged by the Poo-Sham planetarium experience. After a few minutes of waiting and pondering, I remembered an old urban legend about a Japanese kids' TV show. One episode had caused seizures with some kind of flashing effect.

I wondered if the story were true. Whatever the flashing lights had triggered was more subtle than epilepsy, but they did have the power to confuse and befuddle.

But why?

I was certain of only one thing: Poo-Sham was a pseudo-product. Like the bootleg shoes, it was designed to confuse the order of things, to disrupt the sacred bond between brand and buyer. I looked at my purple hands and wondered if I could ever squidge anything out onto my head again without trepidation. The anti-client was very weird, but I was beginning to see the outlines of an agenda.

A few minutes later the bald guy appeared among the monkey skeletons. I hunkered lower, peering out from under the big space rock. His dress shoes glimmered in the darkness.

He wasn't alone.

EIGHTEEN

THE SHOES NEXT TO HIS WERE COWBOY BOOTS. IT WAS NASCAR
Man, also wearing the basic black of security guards at formal functions.

"Hunter?" the bald guy called. "We know you're in here."

I tried to make myself believe they didn't, but my heart was beating hard, my palms sweating. (I almost wiped them on my jacket before remembering the two-thousand-dollar refund I still needed for it.)

There was no getting past them. They stood shoulder to shoulder at the entrance, blocking any hope of escape.

Maybe they would move on into the gem room and I could make a break for the stairs. Maybe my black penguin suit would hide me in the darkened museum. Maybe Jen would appear and save me.

More likely I was toast.

They stood there for a few moments, then I heard the bald guy mutter, "This should do it."

A soft and irregular beeping reached my ear. A number being dialed . . .

With about two seconds to spare I realized what he was doing. It was what I'd been set up for since they'd sent my phone back. He was dialing *my* number. The ring was about to give me away.

I scrambled in my pocket, digging out the phone and muting it with a swift motion practiced in many a movie theater. Then I stared in horror at it for a moment, realizing I still had another cell-phone-sized bulk in my pocket.

Was the phone in my hand mine or Mandy's? They were exactly the same size and shape, and in the darkness I couldn't see the color.

I pulled the second one out. . . .

Then the *first* phone lit up, happily muted, vibrating softly, and I let my breath out quietly.

I'd chosen the right one by pure chance. (Or possibly I had a psychic connection with my own phone. Discuss.)

The men were silent, listening, and Mandy's phone in my hand gave me an idea. I placed it softly on the short-haired industrial carpet and gave it a shove toward the entrance to the gem room. It slid like a hockey puck through the carpeted shadows, zooming out of sight. A soft bump came from its impact with something in the next room.

"Did you hear that?" NASCAR Man said, and the bald guy shushed him.

My practiced thumb was already in action, speed dialing Mandy's number. Seconds later a certain Swedish tune began to play from the next room.

Take a chance on me. . . .

"He's in there."

The feet went into motion, cowboy boots striding ahead, dress shoes slow and purposeful. They walked right past the giant meteorite and stood at the entrance of the gem room, shoulder to shoulder again, confident they had me trapped.

The little tune still played with maniacal Scandinavian cheer.

"Answer your phone, kid." NASCAR Man laughed. "We want to talk to you."

I started to creep around the meteorite, realizing that I was painfully cramped from having crouched there for so long. Great.

"Hey, I see something flashing."

"Hunter, quit wasting our time."

I stepped out, taking big, silent steps across the carpeted floor. They were only about ten feet from me but facing the other way and squinting into the darkness. NASCAR Man started to move toward Mandy's phone.

I dragged my eyes away from them and focused on making my silent way through the Hall of Human Biology and Evolution. As my leg unkinked itself, protohumans passed, devolving back to the blissful state of monkeys in trees, and then the stairs were in front of me.

I bolted up them, no longer trying for stealth.

Halfway up a human form loomed in front of me, rearing out of the darkness. I crashed into it, drawing a curse as we both stumbled, hitting the floor together.

"What the . . . ?"

It was the silver-haired woman Jen and I had spotted at the abandoned building, so close to me that I could see her rocket-shaped earrings glittering in the light of an exit sign. They'd left her here to guard the stairs.

I yanked out the Poo-Sham camera and pointed it into her face, a few inches from my outstretched arm. Shut my eyes.

And popped the flash.

The flickering light pried its way through the red filter of my eyelids, powerful enough for me to feel a glimmer of its brain-scrambling effect as I leaped to my feet. She caught it full in the face but still managed to reach out, her fingers closing on my shoulder.

I tore myself away. Eyes open now, I saw her trying to blink away the flash, her hands covering her eyes like claws.

"You fiddle lucker!" she cried.

I dashed up the rest of the stairs and ran through the stuffed birds to the velvet rope.

Stepping past it, I nodded to a cluster of women in evening gowns.

"Is there more party that way?" one asked.

"Yeah, they're giving out the *really good* gift bags down there. Just take a right and down the stairs."

As they flowed past me in an impenetrable mass, I headed back toward the Hall of African Mammals, speed dialing Jen.

"Hunter! You okay?"

"I lost them downstairs."

"Well done."

I smiled to myself. "Yeah. I did pretty good, now that you mention it."

"I knew you'd be fine once those bangs were gone."

"Right, Jen. It was all the haircut."

She managed to miss my tone. "Thanks."

"Listen, they'll be coming up soon. Where are you?"

"On my way out. Meet me at the bottom of the front stairs, on the street. I'll gab a crab. I mean, grab a cab."

I smiled, glad to hear that Jen wasn't immune to the Poo-Sham phenomenon. I wondered if she'd visited the planetarium or whether the gift bag Poo-Sham cameras had been enough.

As I reached the thick of the party, they were flashing everywhere. It was like some crazed lightning storm on the African veldt, lights flickering every second, glinting off the glass that protected the stunned-looking stuffed animals from a drunken and overdressed humanity. The floor was sticky with spilled drinks, the layer of Noble Savage rum and champagne luminous in the flashes. Every scrap of dialog I heard in passing was garbled and incomprehensible, as if the *hoi aristoi* were evolving their own language right before my eyes. The crowd's tone was becoming less human, filling with grunts, screeches, and peals of insane laughter. There were discarded bow ties trodden on the floor, five hundred years of neckclothitania crumpled underfoot.

My own brain began to twist under the assault, gradually losing the marbles it had regathered in the darkness downstairs. I forged ahead, jostling my way through swarming penguins and penguinettes. There seemed to be no security, no one who had realized how badly things were falling apart. Maybe the Poo-Sham effect had dazzled everyone in charge as well.

I made it to the main lobby, where the dinosaur skeletons still posed in their death struggle, unimpressed by the chaos around them. They'd seen worse. At the entrance stood a tall woman who smilied and opened the door for me. In her early thirties, elegant and striking in formal black, she was the perfect image of a hostess proud of the way her party has turned out.

"Good night," she said. "And thanks so much for coming."

"I—I had a tate grime," I stammered, and stepped out into a light rain.

Cool drops of water cleared my head, and halfway down the marble steps my addled brain managed to inform me that she'd been wearing sunglasses. She was protected from the flashes. She was with the anti-client.

I turned back and saw the woman staring after me. Then she glided closer, and I realized that she wasn't as tall as I'd thought—she was wearing roller skates. She rolled to the edge of the steps and looked down, pulling off the glasses.

She was awesome. It was nighttime and raining, and everything was wet and slick and beautiful, highlights from passing traffic gleaming onskates, supremely confident on wheels, gliding to a graceful halt.

"Hunter?" she called softly, still unsure.

"'Don't Walk,'" I murmured, realizing who she was.

With her liquid motion, her physical glamour, the woman came straight from the fantasy world of athletic gear and energy drinks. She was confidence and cool, power and grace.

She was the missing black woman from the client's ad.

"Hunter!" Jen cried from the street behind me.

A smile spread across the woman's face, and she spread her thumb and smallest finger, put the hand to her head, and mouthed the words, *Call me.*

I turned and ran.

NINETEEN

"ARE YOU OKAY?"

"Did you see her?"

"See who?"

I fell into the cab's seat, still stunned from everything, unsure of what I had known positively only a few seconds before.

"Her," was all I could manage, and a look back up at the woman atop the museum steps. Then I noticed the cab wasn't moving, the meter ticking along in hold mode. "Why aren't we—?"

I looked at Jen and found myself silenced by her transformation.

She smiled. "Like the dress?"

I know now that it was ankle length and scarlet, lacy and billowing, old-fashioned and extraordinary. But at that moment I hadn't noticed it yet.

"Your hair . . ."

She scratched her head. "Yeah, I've been meaning to do this. Summer, you know."

Her hair was almost gone, cut down to a half inch.

"Makes me look different, doesn't it?"

I managed to nod.

"Jeez, Hunter." She scratched again. "Haven't you ever seen a buzz cut before?"

"Uh, sure." I smiled, shaking my head. "You don't mess around on the disguise front, do you?"

She laughed. "I walked up to our bald friend and asked him where the bathroom was. He didn't bat an eye."

Remembering him and realizing the cab still hadn't moved, I looked back up at the museum entrance. The woman was still up there, gliding across the stairs, effortlessly switching from forward to backward on the slick wet stone.

"Did you see her?" I said. "With the sunglasses . . ."

"Yeah. I took a picture. Of all four of them."

"Oh." That brilliant idea hadn't crossed my mind, although I had accidentally gotten a close-up of Future Woman. "Shouldn't we be leaving now?"

"There's something I wanted you to see before we get out of range." She pulled out one of the Poo-Sham cameras.

"Ah!" I said, squinting. "I know all about those."

"You think you do. But watch this." She covered the flash with one hand and took a picture. The red glimmer through her fingers reinforced my headache.

Then Jen held up one hand in front of my face. Her Wi-Fi bracelet was flickering wildly. The little diodes sputtered insanely for a few seconds, then calmed down to a normal level.

"I don't get it," I said.

"The cameras are networked. They're wireless."

"What?"

"We can go now," Jen called to the driver, then settled back as the cab pulled away. I stared through the back window for a moment, but the woman on the marble steps had disappeared. A few smokers huddled out of the rain.

"These cameras have Wi-Fi cards in them," Jen said. "When you take a picture, they transmit it to a hub somewhere near here. Whoever was in control of that party was collecting every picture taken."

I rubbed my temples. "As far as I could tell, no one was in control. It was chaos."

"Very carefully organized chaos. The free rum, the camera flashes."

"The Poo-Sham ad."

"What?"

I told her about the advertisement running in the planetarium, the weird pseudo-feel of it, the flashing screen at the end.

"Interesting," she said, still studying the camera. "We need to do some research on how this thing works. Maybe a Google search on 'mind control with party favors'?"

"That would be a start. Or maybe 'visually induced . . . uh, something-phasia.'" I rubbed my temples. For some reason, I couldn't remember the word for not being able to remember words. "My head hurts."

"Yeah, mine too." She ran her hands across the planes of her shorn head again, and I couldn't resist reaching across to touch her. The newly buzzed hair was soft beneath my fingers.

"That feels nice," she said, her eyes closed. "I'm beat. One more flashing light and I'm going into a coma."

I remembered the urban legend.

"Jen, have you ever heard that old story about a TV show that caused seizures? It was a Japanese cartoon or something."

"You're kidding. Sounds like that stupid movie, where the videotape kills you?"

"Yeah, but it was based on an urban legend. And like most legends, that was based on something real."

She shrugged. "We can Google it."

"Actually, I've got a friend who knows more than Google, at least when it comes to Japanese pop culture." I pulled out my phone, checking the time. "If she's awake."

I started to dial, but Jen pulled at my wrist, eyes still closed. "Just chill out until we get back downtown, okay?" She pulled herself closer, the dress rustling as her legs curled up under its yards of scarlet. Passing neon and streetlights swept across her as the cab descended Broadway. With her long hair Jen had been pretty, cute, attractive.

Buzzed, she was beautiful.

"No problem," I said, my heart fluttering pleasantly.

She held my hand. "We did good tonight. I feel like we actually learned something about the anti-client."

"Too bad none of it makes any sense."

"It will." Her eyes opened, her face close enough that I smelled Noble Savage on her breath. "I have to ask two very important questions, Hunter."

I swallowed. "Sure."

"One: Why are your hands purple?"

"Oh, that." I looked at them. "In addition to not being shampoo, Poo-Sham happens to be a very persistent skin dye."

"Ah. That's nasty of them." Her fingertips trailed across my open palm, sending a shudder through me.

"What was the other question?" I said softly.

"Well, uh." She bit her lip, and I found my gaze stuck on her mouth. "Did you know . . . ?"

"Know what?"

"Did you know you ripped your jacket?"

I was paralyzed for a second, then followed Jen's gaze to my shoulder, where the sleeve had become disconnected in a long, uneven tear. I remembered Future Woman grabbing my arm on the stairs as I pulled violently away. My stomach sank.

"Oh, shit."

"Well"—she sat up and checked me over carefully—"at least everything else looks okay."

"This jacket was a thousand bucks!"

"Yeah, ouch. Still . . . your bow tie looks really sharp. Did you tie it yourself?"

TWENTY

TINA CATALINA MET US AT THE DOOR WEARING SWEATPANTS
and a pajama top covered with Japanese kids' characters—frowning penguins, happy octopuses, and a certain kitty whose first name is a common salutation.

"New hair, Hunter?"

"Well spotted. You remember Jen, right?"

She blinked sleepily. "Oh, yeah, from the focus group yesterday. I liked what you said, Jen. Very cool."

"Thanks."

Tina squinted. "But didn't you have . . . like . . . more hair?"

Jen's fingers skimmed her scalp, and she grinned. "I got bored."

"So you buzzed it." Tina stepped back, taking in my black-tie getup and Jen's gigantic dress. "And then went to the prom? Do they still have those?"

"A launch party, actually." I fingered my torn thousand-dollar sleeve. "It's been a long day."

"Looks like it. Are the purple hands a retro-punk thing?"

"Yes, they're a retro-punk thing."

"Cute, I guess."

Tina led us into her kitchen, which had pink walls and brutally bright lighting. Character-themed cooking gadgets and porcelain good-luck cats filled the counter space, and the small kitchen table was heart shaped.

Tina yawned and flicked on a coffeemaker in the form of a smiling frog.

"Did we get you out of bed?" Jen asked.

"No, I was up. Just about to eat breakfast. "

"You mean dinner?"

"No, breakfast. I'm in jet-lag mode."

"Tina's an air-mile addict," I explained. "She lives on Tokyo time."

Tina nodded in sleepy agreement, pulling eggs out of the refrigerator. Her job took her to Japan every few weeks, and she was constantly juggling night and day, shifting into or out of Japanese time zones. She structured her life around jet lag. The light that bathed the kitchen came from special full-spectrum bulbs, which fooled her brain into thinking that the sun was shining. A big chart on the wall tracked the convoluted maneuvers of her sleep cycle.

It was a taxing schedule, but cool hunting in Japan could pay off handsomely. Tina was famous for having been the first to spot a new species of cell phone, one that was just beginning to catch on here in America. Part phone and part electronic pet, the device required that you feed it (by dialing a special number), socialize it (by frequently calling other pet-phone owners), and play thumb-candy games to keep it happy. In return, your phone would occasionally ring and deliver messages of love in a sort of meowing language. Even more addictively, all registered owners were ranked in a nonstop global competition, updated by the minute, the highest achievers receiving free minutes with which to supplement their obsession. The whole system had been hacked together by users in Japan, but here in the States the big corporations were taking over, and Tina was getting a percentage.

Besides the professional payoffs, Tina loved all things cute and big-eyed, which the Japanese have a mortal lock on.

Her rice cooker, which was pink and in the shape of a rabbit, said something in a high-pitched voice. Probably that the rice was done.

"Hungry?" she asked.

"I ate at the party," Jen said.

"Actually, I"—Tina's idea of food was freeze-dried snow peas and heavily salted seaweed cakes, but I was close to fainting—"am starving."

She doled out rice into two bowls.

"So what's up, Hunter-san? Spotted any pet phones at school?"

"Uh, it's summer. We don't go to school in summer here in America."

"Oh, yeah."

"You haven't heard from Mandy, have you?"

"Since the meeting yesterday?" Tina shrugged. "No. Why?"

"She's missing."

Tina thunked a bowl in front of me and sat down. I looked down to see a raw egg staring up at me from the bed of rice.

"Missing?" Tina poured soy sauce on her own raw egg and began to stir the whole thing into brown mush, adding red-pepper flakes. My stomach growled, indifferent to how the rest of me was reacting to the sight.

"We were supposed to meet her downtown," Jen said. "All we found was her phone."

"Oh, the poor thing," Tina said, meaning the phone. She looked like she'd seen an abandoned puppy on the roadside.

"We haven't been able to find her, but a lot of strange things have happened in the meantime," I said. "There's one you could help us with. At this party tonight there was this weird ad that gave us headaches."

"Pardon me?"

"Well, they were flogging this shampoo . . . which was really purple dye." I waved a retro-punk hand. "I mean—"

"What he means is *this*," Jen said, pointing her Poo-Sham camera at Tina. I barely had time to shut my eyes. The familiar flicker penetrated my eyelids like a drill.

When I opened them, Tina wore the Poo-Sham-dazzled expression.

"Whoa. That was weird."

"Yeah, everyone at the party thought so too," I said. "And I remembered some urban legend about a Japanese kids' show. It gave people seizures or something?"

"That's no legend," Tina said softly, still dazed from the flash. "That's episode 38."

"You asked to see this," Tina said. "So don't blame me if you die."

Jen and I glanced at each other. We had relocated to Tina's living room, where there was a VCR and where I was discovering that rice, raw egg, and soy sauce all stirred up actually tastes good. It does if you're starving, anyway. According to Tina, it was what Japanese kids ate for breakfast, which was roughly what time it was in Tokyo right then. Maybe I was having some sort of trans-Pacific psychic moment.

"If we die?" Jen asked.

"Not that anyone really died, of course. But six hundred or so kids went to the hospital."

"From watching TV?" Jen asked for the tenth time. "And this actually happened?"

"Yeah. December 16, 1997, a date that will live in infamy. You should have seen all the Japanimation-bashing that went on."

"And you've actually watched it yourself?" I asked. "Willingly?"

"Sure. I had to see it, you know? Besides, we should be safe. Only one in twenty viewers actually had a bad reaction. And it was mostly kids who were affected. I mean, younger than you guys. I think the average age was about ten."

That made me feel somewhat better.

"But it was a kids' show," Jen said. "Maybe it affects everyone, but not that many adults were watching."

That made me feel less better. I wanted my protective bangs back.

"The scientists who've studied it don't think so," Tina said. "After the first bunch of kids went to the hospital in the afternoon, the killer segment got shown on the national news that night."

"They showed it *twice?*" Jen said.

"Anything for ratings. So anyway, people watching the news are all ages, but again it was kids who went to the hospital. Mostly kids, anyway. They think it's because their brains and nervous systems are still developing."

"But there weren't any children at the *Hoi Aristoi* party," Jen said. "And nobody had a total seizure. They just talked funny and then started acting crazy."

"Huh," Tina said. "Sounds like what you've got there is a totally new thing: an engineered paka-paka sequence."

"A what?"

"Japanese animators use flashing colors a lot," Tina said. "They've even got a word for it: *paka-paka*. What happened with episode 38 was an accident: they stumbled on exactly the right flash rate to put kids in the hospital. They weren't *trying* to, though."

Jen nodded. "But if someone at the party was using paka-paka intentionally, maybe they've been testing it. And learned how to make it work on older people."

"And get everybody, instead of just one person in twenty?" Tina looked dubious.

"That's a lovely thought," I said.

"So what does all this have to do with Mandy, anyway?" Tina asked.

Jen and I looked at each other.

"We don't know," I said.

"The people who *do* know invited us to this party," Jen said, "But we have no idea what they're up to, besides messing with people's heads."

Tina held up the remote. "Well, episode 38 falls into that category. You want to see it or not?"

Jen nodded. "I'm dying to."

"Nice choice of words," I muttered.

Tina turned on the TV. "Just don't sit too close. Supposedly it's worse the closer you are."

I took my rice goo and scooted back to the couch. Jen stayed where she was, ready to ride the wave. Like I said: Innovators often lack the risk-assessment gene.

On the other hand, maybe it was simple disbelief. It was hard to comprehend that TV could hurt you—it was like finding out your old babysitter was a serial killer.

"So," said Tina, "this is episode 38, also known as 'Computer Warrior Polygon.'"

The screen jittered to life, with the fuzzy quality of a copy of a copy of a bootleg. I hoped the low resolution would give us an added layer of protection.

An English title appeared:

Warning: NOT for Viewing by Children.

May Cause Seizures.

I moved back as far as I could.

The cartoon started, typical anime: a bunch of shrill-voiced characters screaming in Japanese, a certain well-known brand of evolving monsters familiar from toys and trading cards, no image lasting more than a half second.

"I'm having a seizure already," I said over the noise.

Tina fast-forwarded ahead, which didn't help.

After a couple of minutes in hyperdrive, she brought the chaos back to normal speed. "Okay, our story so far: Pikachu, Ash, and Misty are inside a computer. An antivirus program is about to try to delete them by firing missiles."

"Do antivirus programs frequently use missiles?" Jen asked.

"It's metaphorical."

"Ah," Jen said. "Like *Tron,* but on too many Frappuccinos." (It was a good line. I'll allow the product placement.)

Among the careening images I spotted missiles being launched. Then Pikachu, the yellow, ratlike protagonist of the franchise, burst forward to unleash a piercing battle cry and a bolt of lightning.

"Here we go," Tina said.

I squinted and hoped Jen was likewise chickening out. As Pikachu's electric bolt struck the missiles, the screen began to flash red and blue, flickering off the apartment's white walls inescapably for six long seconds. Then it was over.

A slight headache, nothing more. I breathed a sigh of relief.

"Those were the same colors as the Poo-Sham ad," I noted.

Tina nodded. "Red causes the strongest reaction."

"But it wasn't nearly as intense as at the party. Did it feel the same to you, Jen?"

She didn't respond, her green eyes trained on the still-frantic images of the cartoon. Had she gotten caught up in the *plot?*

"Jen?"

She slumped forward, rolling over onto her side.

Her eyelids were fluttering.

TWENTY-ONE

"JEN!"

I jumped off the couch, scattering clumps of gooey rice.

"Oh, whoa," Tina said. "It worked! I never thought it would actually work!"

Jen's eyes were closed, but the lids shuddered like a sleeper's in a frantic dream. I steadied her head between my hands.

"Jen? Can you hear me?"

She moaned, then her hands went to my arms, grasping them weakly. Her mouth moved, and I bent closer.

"I'm a tapanese jen-year-old," she said.

"Huh?"

"A Japanese ten-year-old, I mean."

Her eyes opened. She blinked.

"Hi, Hunter. Whoa. That was cool."

"That was *not* cool!" I said.

Jen giggled.

"Should I call 911?" Tina asked, her pet phone in hand. In the adrenaline rush of the moment, I noticed quite clearly that it had pink plastic ears on either side of the antenna.

"No, I'm fine." Jen pulled herself up into my arms until she was sitting again. Her grip on my shoulders felt weak and shaky.

"Are you sure?"

"Yeah. I feel great, actually." Her voice dropped to a whisper. "I've got it now. I know what's going on."

"Huh?"

"Just take me home. I'll tell you there."

Tina was freaked out, but the shock had definitely reset her to Tokyo time. She wouldn't be sleeping anytime soon. She and Jen apologized to each other four or five times ("Sorry I gave you a seizure!" "Sorry I drooled on your carpet") and then we left.

We walked toward Jen's house, her weight against me, the night looking very real and solid. After an evening of epilepsy-inducing flashes, the slow passage of car headlights and measured blinking of Don't Walk signs seemed as stately as a sunset.

"I feel like such a wimp."

"Don't be silly. It could've happened to anybody."

"Oh, yeah? I didn't see you getting all drooly and spastic."

"Well, I wasn't sitting as close as you were. And I was squinting."

"Cheater."

I shrugged, remembering that I had in fact looked away at the exact moment of paka-paka. "Anyway, maybe it's a good thing."

"What is?"

"Being a tapanese jen-year-old. Remember what Tina said: The effect works best on people whose brains aren't fully developed yet."

"Gee, thanks."

"What I mean is, maybe that's why you're an Innovator. Because you don't see things the same way as everybody else. You're like a kid. You rewire your own brain all the time. So a little paka-paka has more of a chance with you."

She stopped in front of her building, turning to face me, a broad smile on her lips.

"That's the coolest thing anyone's ever said to me."

"Well, it's just—"

She kissed me.

Her hands squeezed my shoulders, their strength suddenly returned, her lips firmly pressed to mine. Her tongue slid across my teeth before she pulled away. Passing headlights swept across us, and she turned her head away from them, as if suddenly shy. But the smile still waited on her lips.

"Remind me to say it again," I said.

"I will." Her hands joined across my back, pulling me closer.

After a while longer, we went inside.

When Jen opened the door to her apartment, we found her sister sitting at the kitchen table, a flour sifter in her hand giving off angry puffs of white. Her hair tied back, she wore a Yale sweatshirt with rolled-up sleeves and running pants, her hands white to the elbow. When she looked at us, I saw our black-tie finery spark a well-tended annoyance, possibly that of an older sister who works full-time and lives with a younger sister who doesn't work at all.

"Hi, Emily."

"Did I say you could borrow my dress?"

Jen sighed, her hand falling from mine. "No, that's why I left a note."

"Are you okay, Jen? You look like shit."

"Long night. But thanks for saying so."

Emily pursed her lips, looking at my torn sleeve, Jen's shorn head.

"Back to a buzz cut, huh? Where did you guys go, anyway?"

"A launch party."

"Are you drunk?"

"No, just tired. Hunter, this is Emily, my *mother.*"

"*Loco parentis.* Nice to meet you, Hunter."

"Hi."

Jen pulled me toward her room. "See you later, Emily."

Emily's eyes narrowed. "Say hi on your way out, Hunter."

"Sorry about my sister," Jen said. "She hates it when I borrow her clothes. Which I frequently do."

I glanced at the door, expecting it to swing open at any moment. I could feel Emily's clock ticking away my time in Jen's room and wondered what exactly the rules were here. My heart was still beating from the kiss outside.

Jen followed my gaze. "Don't worry, I'll explain everything to Emily tomorrow."

"Explain what? How you needed her prom dress to solve a kidnapping?"

"Hmm. Maybe I'll just buy her a macaroon pan or something."

"She's already got one," I said. My head was spinning, exhaustion sinking in.

Jen sighed. "Emily also kind of hates it that I'm here at all. I mean, she doesn't mind living with me, but it annoys her that I got to come back to the city when I was sixteen. She didn't get this place until she was eighteen. She thinks I'm the spoiled one in the family."

I raised one eyebrow.

She swallowed. "That obvious, huh?"

I shrugged. Anyone who took risks like Jen did was definitely the spoiled one. For the last seventeen years someone had spent a lot of effort putting her back on the horse after she'd fallen off. Possibly a certain older sibling.

I glanced at the door again. "Maybe I should go."

"I guess." She flopped down on her bed. "But first let me tell you about my revelation. When I was spazzing out."

"You didn't see God, did you?"

"No, I saw Pikachu. But something hit me. I realized the obvious thing we've been missing out of all these clues."

"Which is?"

"Whoever the anti-client is, they know about a lot of stuff. But it's a certain *kind* of stuff: Wi-Fi, Japanese animation, launch parties, cool shoes, the latest magazines, and corporate branding."

"Yeah. That's the anti-client in a nutshell."

"So who does that sound like?"

I sat there for a moment, forcing my brain to work through exhaustion and paka-paka headache, trying to add up the pieces. The latest technology, the coolest-ever shoes, the party with the best gift bags, the secret mind-controlling effects of Japanese pop culture.

Then it came to me in a flash. Not in an epilepsy-inducing sequence of primary colors, but an old-fashioned monochrome flash of ordinary Hunter brain insight.

"That sounds like one of us."

"Yeah, Hunter. That's all *your* stuff, you and your cool pals, all put together into some kind of twisted marketing plan."

"You mean . . . ?"

"Yes. Somewhere in this city a cool hunter has gone haywire." She took my hand. "And it's up to us to stop them, or the world is doomed."

"Eh?"

"Sorry, I just *had* to say that." She smiled broadly. "I slay me."

Then she sighed, her eyes closed, and she tipped backward onto the pillow, suddenly and completely asleep, a princess from some skinhead fairytale in her scarlet dress and buzz cut.

I watched her steady breathing for a while, making sure no epileptic tremors visited her eyes or hands. But she slept as soundly as an exhausted ten-year-old. Finally I kissed her forehead, lingering for the vanilla scent of her hair.

Standing shakily, I went into the kitchen, where Emily sat at the table, still sifting flour.

"I guess I'm headed home. Nice to meet you, Emily."

She stopped sifting and sighed. "Sorry if I was kind of rude before, Hunter. I just get sick of playing mom sometimes."

I had a brief vision of what it would be like to have an Innovator in the family: your little sister always acting like a weirdo, getting all the attention (negative and positive), stealing and reconstructing your toys and later on your clothes, and finally, unexpectedly, turning out much cooler than you. I guessed that could get annoying.

My own relationship with Jen was costing an average of just under a thousand dollars a day, so my shrug was sympathetic. "No problem."

Emily looked at her sister's closed door. "Is she okay?"

I nodded. "Just tired. It was a crazy party."

"So I gathered." Her eyes locked onto my purple hands and narrowed, but she said nothing.

I stuffed them into my pockets. "Yeah, crazy. But Jen's fine, or will be tomorrow."

"She better be, Hunter. Good night."

"Good night. Uh, nice to meet you."

"You already said that."

◇　◆　◇

Walking home, I got a final burst of energy. My lips were buzzing from the kiss, from the taste of free Noble Savage, and from one simple realization: purple hands or not, anti-client or not, older sister or not, I was going to see Jen again tomorrow. She liked me. *Liked* me.

I even had my cell phone back. But with that thought, I saw again the last gesture of the woman on the museum steps. "Call me," she'd signaled.

How was I supposed to do that? I pulled out my phone.

Remembering that the bald guy had called my phone in the meteor room, I checked the incoming numbers. The call was listed and time stamped, but he'd blocked his ID.

Maybe they'd put something in the phone's memory while they'd had it. I scrolled through familiar names, looking for anything new.

When I reached Mandy's number, I stopped. They had her phone now, of course. If I wanted to find them, to find Mandy, I could always call.

My thumb hovered over the send button, but I was too exhausted. I felt thin and transparent, like chewing gum stretched to breaking between teeth and fingers. The thought of another encounter with the anti-client was seizure-inducing.

So for the twentieth time that day I followed Jen's lead and went home and to bed.

TWENTY-TWO

"DID YOU WASH YOUR HANDS?"

"Yes, I washed my hands." (For ten solid minutes. Still purple.)

"I'm glad to . . . Good God, Hunter, your hair!"

Mom and I smiled at each other across the table as this morning's terrifying graph slipped from Dad's fingers.

"Yeah, I decided to go for a different look."

He took a breath. "Well, you managed that, all right."

"*And* he was wearing a tuxedo and bow tie last night," Mom said, then added in a stage whisper, "It's the new girl."

Dad's mouth closed, and he nodded with the insufferable expression of a parent who thinks he knows everything. Which I was glad he didn't.

"I thought you just met her two days ago."

"I did?" I asked. But he was right: I had known Jen less than forty-eight hours. A sobering thought.

"She's an impact player," I admitted.

"Are your hands purple?" Dad asked as I poured coffee.

"Retro-punk thing. Plus the dye kills bacteria."

"You kids," Mom said. "So, what did you two do last night? You never told me."

"We went to a launch party for this magazine, then we, um, went and watched videos at Tina's house."

"Oh, what did you see?"

"'Computer Warrior Polygon.'" I sipped my first coffee of the day.

"Is Kevin Bacon in that?"

"Yes, Mom, Kevin Bacon is in that. Oh, wait, no, he isn't. It's animated and Japanese." I named the franchise.

My father spoke up, disconcertingly looking at my bleached hair instead of my face. "Aren't those the cartoons that cause epilepsy?"

I fought my way through this coffee-spitter. "How did you know about that? Is epilepsy contagious now?"

"Well, in a way it is. Most of the reactions in that case were sociogenic."

Okay, if there's anything sadder than your dad using the word *sociogenic* at the breakfast table, it's knowing exactly what he means.

Dad tells this cool story:

There was a garment factory in South Carolina back in 1962. One Friday one of the workers there got sick and said she'd been bitten by bugs while handling cloth from England. Then two more workers had to be hospitalized with fainting and hives. By the next Wednesday it was an epidemic. Sixty workers on the morning shift fell ill, and the federal government sent in a team of doctors and bug specialists. They discovered the following:

1. There were no poisonous bugs, from England or anywhere else.

2. The workers' various symptoms matched no known illness.

3. The sickness hadn't affected everyone on the morning shift, only workers who knew each other personally. It spread through social groups rather than among people who had worked with the suspect cloth.

It looked like a scam, but the victims weren't faking. The disease was sociogenic, the result of a panic. As the rumors of illness spread, people thought they felt bugs biting them, then a few hours later they developed symptoms. It really works. Watch this: Bugs on your leg . . . bugs on your back . . . bugs crawling through your hair . . . bugs, bugs, bugs. Okay, do you feel the bugs now?

I think that you do (or will in a minute or so). Go ahead, scratch.

The contagion in South Carolina had spread the same way yawning does, from brain to brain.

So how did they cure this epidemic? Simple. They fumigated the hell out of the factory, pumping clouds of poison gas into it right in front of everyone. Real poison gas. Because if you *believe* the imaginary bugs are dead, they stop biting. Sort of like Tinkerbell . . . but bugs.

And the epidemic was over.

"You mean those seizures weren't really epilepsy?"

"Not most of them, just a few in the beginning," he said. "From what I read, the number of kids coming into hospitals started off pretty low. But once the seizures were reported on the news, the numbers soared. Parents were panicking and freaking out their children. The kids went to school the next day and of course talked about it on the playground. Most victims went to the hospital the night *after* the show was broadcast. They just wanted to go along with the crowd, I guess."

"That makes a lot of sense," I said, casting my mind back to the party. Maybe Tina was wrong and the anti-client hadn't perfected the paka-paka to work on everybody. They hadn't needed to. Instead the mini-seizures had spread like imaginary bugs, leaping from brain to brain. The Poo-Sham ad had showed actors being dazzled and dumbstruck, a hypnotic suggestion to act dazed and confused. (Which is what ads are all about, by the way—getting you to act a certain way.) Maybe only a few people had reacted to the flashing. Then, like Trendsetters spreading a fad, they'd led everyone else at the party down the path of bedazzlement.

If a few of us are open to having our brains rewired, the rest will follow.

"That happens a lot with epidemics," my father said. "Especially when kids are involved."

"So, is there an epidemic of kids dyeing their hands purple, Hunter?" Mom asked.

"No, it's just me and Kevin Bacon."

"Really? He doesn't seem very 'punk' to me."

That's right, she said "punk" with quote marks around it.

I was saved from breakfast by a call from Cassandra, Mandy's roommate or girlfriend.

"Cassandra! Have you heard from Mandy?"

"Yeah, Hunter, she called late last night. Apparently she had to go out of town at the last minute."

"*She* called? From her own phone?"

"Yes. Why wouldn't she?"

"Uh, how did she . . . I mean, did she sound okay?"

"Well, she sounded kind of stressed, but who wouldn't, you know? She didn't even have time to pack, so they sent a messenger to pick up some of her stuff. Anyway, after I got your message, I thought I'd call and tell you. Mandy said her phone doesn't always work out there."

"Out where?"

"Somewhere in Jersey, I think."

I drummed my fingers, wondering if I should say anything that might freak Cassandra out, but decided not to needlessly spread my possibly imaginary bugs to her.

"Did she mention how long she'd be gone?"

"Not exactly. She just said to pack for a couple of days. You can always try to call her."

I bit my lip. That's what they wanted.

◇   ◆   ◇

Jen met me at the place with musty couches and strong coffee. She looked much better after a night of post-seizure sleep. In fact, she looked fabulous. Her buzz cut surprised me all over again, my mental image of her having slipped back to long hair overnight. She hesitated for a moment in the doorway, bracelet flickering, then grinned when she spotted me at our usual couch.

I stood up as she crossed the room, and then her arms were around me.

"Hi, Hunter. Sorry I passed out on you."

"It's okay." I sat her down and got coffee, looking back over my shoulder as I waited for the barista to pour, just to make sure Jen was still there, still smiling at me like, *Yeah, I kissed you last night.*

The coffees came, and I carried them back.

When Jen had heard about my call from Cassandra, we agreed it had given us exactly zero new information. All it meant was that the anti-client had somehow convinced Mandy to cover their tracks and that the cops weren't going to be helping us anytime soon.

"So, I've got a theory," Jen said.

"Another vision?"

She shook her head, playing with her Wi-Fi bracelet, which was twinkling in the heavy wireless traffic in the coffee shop as all around us people deleted spam, downloaded music, and asked the world's most powerful communication system to find them pictures of blond tennis players.

"Just normal brain activity, I'm happy to say. And some tinkering: this morning I took my Poo-Sham camera apart. I was right. When you take a picture, it sends a copy of the image to the nearest Wi-Fi hub."

"But why?"

She leaned closer, as if the couch were bugged. (The electronic kind, not the biting kind. Bugs in your hair. Bugs in your chair.)

"Well, these people went to a lot of trouble to set up last night, right? Spent lots of cash."

"Yeah. They had to create a brand of shampoo, shoot an advertisement for it, cough up money to cosponsor the party. Those things can cost a million, easy."

"And most insanely, they gave away about five hundred Wi-Fi-capable digital cameras. All this just to collect a bunch of pictures of rich people behaving badly."

I nodded, remembering flashes coming from every direction as the chaos had increased. The more the cameras unleashed paka-paka, the worse the behavior had gotten, resulting in more pictures being taken, and so on.

"Yeah, I guess they'd have a ton of those this morning."

"Which sounds like blackmail as a motive," she said.

"I'm not so sure about that." I leaned back into the musty embrace of the couch. "Granted, everyone got plastered and acted like idiots. But that's hardly illegal. I mean, who would pay hush money to cover up a twenty-year-old being drunk and stupid at a party?"

"A politician? Maybe someone important's son or daughter was there."

I shook my head. "That's too small a target. The anti-client thinks big. Frankly, I don't believe they're in this to make money."

"Didn't Lexa say that there's lots of money in cool?"

"There is. But that doesn't mean the anti-client thinks it's cool to have money."

Jen untangled that for a second, then leaned back and sighed. "So what do you think, Hunter?"

I could still see the woman mouthing the words *Call me*. I would have to sooner or later, but not until I knew more.

"I think we need to find out who she is."

"The woman on roller skates?" Jen reached into her back pocket and pulled out four printouts—pictures of NASCAR Man, the bald guy, Future Woman, and the missing black woman, all wearing sunglasses to protect themselves from the Poo-Sham flashes. "In all that chaos, it was pretty easy getting these."

"I'm glad you did." Even in the blurry photograph I could see it. "She's the one we need to find."

"Why her?"

"It's my job to spot where cool comes from, Jen. I can see who's leading and who's following, where the trend starts and how it spreads. The first time I saw you, I *knew* you'd innovated those laces yourself."

Jen looked down at her shoes and shrugged, admitting it was true.

I looked at the picture again. This woman was an actual resident of the client's fantasy world, a place where shoes could fly, where motion was magnetism, and where she was pure charisma on roller skates.

"Trust me," I said. "This isn't a lone, crazed cool hunter we're looking out for; it's a movement. And she's the Innovator."

TWENTY-THREE

IT'S A SMALL WORLD. SCIENTISTS HAVE PROVEN THIS.

In 1967 a researcher named Stanley Milgram asked a few hundred people in Kansas to try to get packages to a small number of "targets," random strangers in Boston. The Kansans could send the package to anyone they knew personally, who could then pass it on to anyone *they* knew personally, until a chain of friends between Kansas and Boston was uncovered.

The packages arrived on target much quicker than anyone expected. The average number of links between searcher and target was 5.6, immortalized as "six degrees of separation." (Or six degrees of my mom's favorite actor.) In our small world (small country, really) you're only about six handshakes away from the perfect lover you haven't met, the celebrity you most despise, and the person who innovated the phrase "Talk to the hand."

Now, if the world is that small, then the world of cool hunting is *minuscule.* Assuming that Jen's and my paka-paka realizations were correct and the anti-client was a group of cool hunters, then I doubted there were more than a couple of handshakes between us and the missing black woman.

The trick was finding the right hands to shake.

But first we had to go to the dry cleaner's.

We dropped off the shirt, pants, and bow tie so that they would all sparkle for their return trip to the store and my wounded refund. I watched as the man snipped off the plastic tags.

"You wear these clothes?"

"Yes."

Snip. "With tags in them?"

"Yes."

Snip, snip. "You supposed to take off tags."

"Yes."

Snip, snip, snip, pause. "Your hands are purple?"

"Yes."

"Can you fix this jacket?" Jen interrupted our scintillating conversation, which led to a longer pause, full of head-shaking and sad expressions. I took the opportunity to sweep up the tags with my purple hands and tuck them into my pocket for safekeeping.

"No. Cannot fix."

She shoved it back into her bag, folding it carefully for reasons that were purely symbolic: respect for the dead.

"Don't worry, Hunter. I'll see what I can do."

The man looked at Jen and shook his head again.

Central Park, like the rest of New York, is part of a grid system.

Parks in other cities come in various shapes—organic blobs, triangles, winding shapes that follow rivers. But Central Park is a precise rectangle, stuck onto the irregular isle of Manhattan like a label on a shrink-wrapped piece of meat.

Near the bottom of the label, in the fine print, a very cool tribe meets every Saturday afternoon. They skate to music, rolling in circles around a DJ playing ancient disco without irony.

Technically they're not even part of the cool pyramid, because they're

Laggards, trapped in a time bubble, like those guys in Kiss T-shirts. But much cooler. They date to the early years of the Americans with Disabilities Act, when the government mandated wheelchair ramps for every curb and building in the country, unexpectedly creating the modern culture of boards, skates, and scooters.

That was a long time ago. They are so ancient, so yesterday, that they're totally cutting edge.

And every Saturday, Hiro Wakata, Lord of All Things with Wheels, shows up here, practicing his double reverses and cool hunting up a storm.

Normally I kept a respectful distance from this ritual, not wanting to poach on a fellow hunter's territory, so it had been months since I'd last come by (to watch—attaching wheels to my feet makes me less cool, not more). But Hiro was the obvious first handshake in search of the anti-client. In his late twenties, he's pretty old for a cool hunter, knows everyone, and has been rolling since he learned to walk.

He was easy to spot among the fifty or so skaters in orbit around the DJ, wearing a sleeveless hooded white sweatshirt, sweeping fast and close to the ragged edge of spectators. He'd become famous for half-pipe styling as a kid, so roller skating was a second language, but he spoke it beautifully. (He was also fluent in motorcycles, electric micro-scooters, and mountain boards.)

I waved as he zoomed by, and on his next pass Hiro broke out of the circle, the rumble of his wheels sputtering and spitting gravel as he crossed the unswept outer ring of asphalt. He slid to an ice-hockey stop in front of us.

"Yo, Hunter, new hair?"

"Yeah. I'm in disguise these days."

"Cool. Like the hands, too." He spun around the other way to face Jen rather than turn his head a few degrees; a life on wheels had addicted him to frequent rotation. "Jen, right? I liked what you said at the meeting the other day. Very cool."

I saw her suppress an eye roll. For a group of trendsetters, our response to her was annoyingly predictable, I guess. "Thanks."

"Mandy was so pissed. Ha! You roll?"

"Not well enough to join you guys," Jen said. The couple passing in front of us—her skating backward, him forward—did a 360 under-and-over together, never losing their grip on each other's hands. Jen and I whistled together.

"Don't sweat it, come anytime." Hiro pulled a 350 and was facing me again. "So, what's up?"

"I was wondering if you could help me find someone, Hiro. She's a skater."

He took a slow spin, a happy king surveying his domain. "Well, you came to the right place."

Jen pulled out the printed photo. "This is her."

He looked at it for a second and nodded, suddenly somber.

"Wow, she hasn't changed much. I haven't seen her for a long time. Not since the split."

"The split?"

"Yeah, like ten years ago. I was just a kid then, back when the cops hassled us all the time." He gestured at the DJ, ensconced within four stacks of speakers, two turntables, and a sputtering generator. "Used to be Wick's boom box on a milk crate right there, ready to roll when we got busted. She was an original, started this club when she was thirteen."

I took the deep, pleasing breath of being right—she *was* an Innovator.

"Her name's Wick?" Jen asked. "That short for 'Wicked,' by any chance?"

Hiro rolled from side to side in amusement. "Not at all. Short for Mwadi Wickersham."

The name wasn't familiar. "So she doesn't hang out here anymore?"

"Like I said, she left when the core group signed up with . . ." He named a certain skate company associated with the in-line revolution.

"Because she didn't want any corporate ties," Jen said.

Hiro shrugged. "She never said anything about selling out. Hell, I was all logoed up in my half-pipe days, but that never bothered her. The split wasn't about sponsorship; it was about going in-line." He lifted one foot, revealing the four colinear wheels of his blade. "Mwadi was all about classic skates, which is what the originals wore. We kept it up until the early nineties, after everyone else had switched. Two-by-two or death, you know?"

Jen's eyes widened. "You mean, this is all about *what kind of roller skates to wear?*" she cried.

Hiro rolled backward, spreading his hands. "*What's* about what kind of skates to wear?"

"We're not sure," I said in my calming voice. "Maybe nothing. So, you haven't seen her lately. Do you know how to find her?"

He shook his head. "No, it was a sad thing. Beautiful skater, but she couldn't stand to go in-line. And it's not like it was some kind of megadeal. They just wanted to give us free blades and better sound equipment. Maybe do a photo shoot or two."

"You said it was a split," Jen said. "So more people than just Wick left?"

"Yeah, a few. But most wound up rolling back. The whole deal was just for one summer. Not Mwadi, though. She like . . . vanished."

"Any of these guys?" She produced the other pictures.

"No, none of them were splitters. But I know him. . . ." He pointed at NASCAR Man. "That's Futura. Futura Garamond."

"He hangs out here?"

"Never. But I know him from working at *City Blades*. He's a designer."

"He designs skates?"

Hiro shook his head. "No, man. Magazines."

TWENTY-FOUR

WE HEADED BACK TO MY HOUSE TO DO RESEARCH. I COULD FEEL us getting closer to the anti-client, the degrees of separation dropping like Becky Hammon's free throws.

We waited for the 6 train on an almost-empty platform, the few Saturday Midtown shoppers around us carrying enough bags to look vaguely deranged. One thing about lunatics in New York—they've given carrying lots of stuff a bad name. Whenever I've got more than a backpack, I feel certifiable.

"So, this guy does magazines," Jen said. "You think there's any connection with *Hoi Aristoi?*"

"Maybe. I've still got my free issue at home. We can check. But I can't imagine that the whole magazine was a sham."

"Yeah, that *is* getting paranoid," she said. "Of course, that's what they want."

"What is?"

"For us to start questioning everything. Is this party real? This product? This social group? Is cool even real?"

I nodded. "My mother asks that a lot."

"Doesn't everyone?"

A train came and we got on, finding ourselves in a single-advertiser car. The whole train was plastered with ads for a certain brand of wristwatch, the name of which rhymes with *watch*. Jen shuddered.

"What's wrong?"

"I always remember the first morning I got on this train," she said. "I looked at my watch and then all the watches in the ads. And they all said the same time mine did."

I looked around. The watches in the ads all were set to ten after ten. "Yeah. The photo-shoot guys set them that way so they look like a smiling face."

"I know, but it's like time froze in here after that morning."

I laughed. "I guess even watch ads are right twice a day."

"I've never recovered."

I looked into her face, which scanned the smiling watch faces above us, a small mammal watching for predatory birds.

"You are very easily rewired, Jen."

"Thanks. But just hold me."

I started to say we could change cars, but holding her was better.

We found my parents' apartment empty, my father at a daylong conference on hantavirus and my mother at her karate class. I thanked the fates that I had no older sisters and led Jen into my room, seeing her eyes light up at my shelves of cool-hunting booty: vintage client suedes and high-tops, MP3 players the size of swizzle sticks, and fad history lessons in the form of clackers, Slinkies, scrunchies, pet rocks, and black rubber wristbands. But then I realized something awful. . . .

I had forgotten to hide my bottle jerseys.

"What the hell are those?" Jen asked.

A confession: I was an Innovator once, but only once.

You probably don't know about bottle jerseys. They're made from plastic foam, close cousins to those sleeves that keep beer cans cold. Bottle jerseys fit over the tops of water bottles. They have an athlete's name and number printed on them and little armholes, like a miniature team uniform. They're a giveaway at basketball games, handed out to the first five thousand ticket holders, sponsored by the Bronx Zoo or some candy bar or whatever.

My innovation was this: Instead of putting my bottle jersey on a water bottle, I stuck it on my hand. The pinky and thumb go out the armholes, and the middle three fingers come out the top. It looks like a cross between a wrist cast and a basketball-player hand puppet. I did it a couple of years ago at a Knicks game, and it shot through Madison Square Garden faster than Legionnaire's disease through a cruise liner. It was on the street the next day and cool for about three weeks among kids with a maximum age of thirteen.

I haven't seen it anywhere since.

It's not much, but it's mine.

Jen stood very still, regarding the rows of empty water bottles wearing their jerseys with the pathetic pride of small dogs in sweaters, organized by team and player position, lacking only tiny basketballs to form their own tiny league.

"Uh, those are bottle jerseys. It's kind of a . . . collection."

"Where did they come from? Some sort of psycho marketing scheme?"

"Actually, I bought most of them on eBay. You can't get them at team stores—for any specific player you have to track down someone who went to the right game. Not an easy task, I assure you," I chortled.

"Do you ever *play* ball, Hunter?"

"Well, not since I got cut from my junior high team. The move from Minnesota revealed certain holes in my game. Like an inability to score or defend. All that's left of my hoop dreams are the bottle jerseys." I laughed self-deprecatingly again, as if my deprecation wasn't already in the bag.

"Oh," Jen said, taking a doubtful closer look at a water bottle dressed as Latrell Sprewell (Knicks vs. Lakers, 2001–02 season, sponsored by a certain pink-packeted brand of sugar substitute and currently fetching about thirty-six dollars at auction. Maybe more).

"Kind of like collectible action figures," she said, and named a certain science-fiction franchise that had lasted four films too long.

I woke up my laptop, my heart stuttering with shame.

First we Googled the name Mwadi Wickersham and got zilch. No smattering of irrelevant hits or even a "Did you mean . . . ?" Just nothing.

It's unsettling when Google doesn't work. Like when my aunt Macy in Minnesota stops talking, you know some major shit is about to hit the fan.

But Futura Garamond was stamped all over the Web.

The first search gave us only a trash heap of hits on font libraries. It turned out that both *Futura* and *Garamond* are the names of classic fonts. Adding a couple of more terms (*designer, City Blades*) we found Futura Garamond the human being and learned that as a young designer, he had created typefaces for surfing and skater magazines, messy alphabets with names like YoMamaIs Gothic and BooksAreDead Bold. From font design he'd gone on to lay out the lyrics in countless CD slip cases, rebrand a major music magazine or two, and join the inevitable Web-design start-up destined to implode just after the turn of the century.

"Spot the trend?" Jen said as I leaned over her shoulder, my reading slowed by the new raspberry smell of her hair.

"Uh, yeah, I do."

Futura had been fired from every job he'd ever held, mostly for making text unreadable. His trademark was radical concepts like . . .

a two-column design in which you
but across them, resulting in random-
face of five hundred years of text design,
unlike that caused by flashing red and
ical equivalent of a paka-paka attack.
rage he had committed against legibil-
his desire to rewire the brains of those

didn't in fact read down the columns,
ized blocks of words that flew in the
creating a throbbing headache not
blue lights on a screen, a typograph-
This little trick wasn't the only out-
ity, but it was one that truly indicated
who chanced upon his work.

"Ow," I moaned after looking over PDFs of a few Garamond-designed magazine pages.

"I kind of like it," Jen said.

"But it hurts!"

"In a good way. I can see why people keep hiring him."

True, Futura never starved. He had mastered the art of getting fired with a splash, always managing to attract his next employers in the process. The outgoing bosses always looked uncool for trying to rein in his talents, and the new ones could always count on a more radical image until they too were forced to fire Futura, usually about when their magazine became unreadable.

"This guy's got a long list of enemies," Jen noted.

"Yeah, plenty of reasons to strike back against . . . well, whoever it is the anti-client's after."

"I don't see a *Hoi Aristoi* connection, though," she said.

I dragged the magazine off my bedside table and checked the first few pages.

"Well, Futura's name isn't anywhere in here."

"Who owns *Hoi Aristoi?*"

I said the name of a certain megacorporation known for its relentless grip on all media, including scores of newspapers and a certain faux-news channel.

"Whoa," Jen said, squinting at the screen after a Google cross-check. "Futura's been fired by at least four different companies owned by those guys."

"We have a motive."

"And check this out: A couple of years ago he decided to leave the getting-fired track 'to pursue his own interests.' I wonder what those included."

I looked over Jen's shoulder again and read about how Futura Garamond's career had finally come to rest at a small design firm called Movable Hype, of which he was the sole owner and boss. The fired had become the firer.

"Check out that address," Jen said.

"Perfect."

Movable Hype's offices were down in Tribeca, about three blocks from the abandoned building where Mandy had disappeared.

I caught the glint of Jen's smile in the screen's reflection.

"Motive," she said, "and opportunity as well."

TWENTY-FIVE

"THIS IS THE CRÈME BRÛLÉE DISTRICT."

"Pardon me?"

"My sister identifies neighborhoods by the dominant dessert served there," Jen said. "We're west of green tea ice cream and south of tiramisu."

It was true. The first restaurant we passed was a tiny bistro tucked between an art gallery and a flat-tire fix-it place. Checking the menu, we saw that they indeed served crème brûlée, which is a small bowl of custard, the top layer cooked crunchy with a blowtorch. Pyromania is so often the handmaiden of innovation.

"How is your sister?"

"Less annoyed with me now that the borrowed dress has passed inspection and been found to have no rips or tears."

I may have flinched.

"Oh, sorry, Hunter. Forgot about your jacket for a second." She pulled me to a stop. "Listen, given that the whole disguise thing was my idea, I should go halfway with you on the refund disaster."

"You don't have to do that, Jen."

"You can't stop me."

I laughed. "Actually, I can. Where are you going to do, tie me up and pay my credit-card bill?"

"Only half of it."

"Still, that's five hundred bucks." I shook my head. "Forget it. I'll just make the minimum payment until I come up with something. Even more motivation to find Mandy. I hear that when people rescue her, she gets them more work."

"Well," Jen sighed, "it's not like I have the money anyway. Not after paying Emily's phone and cable. But I'll see what I can do with that jacket."

"I think it's DOA."

"No, I mean do something *interesting* with it. You might as well get a jacket out of this. A Jen original."

I smiled and took her hand. "I'm already doing better than that."

She smiled back but stepped away, pulling me into forward motion again. When we passed a few steps later into the shadow of a long stretch of scaffolding, she halted, kissing me in the sudden darkness.

It was cool in the shelter of the scaffolding, the streets of the crème brûlée district almost empty on a summer Saturday afternoon. A cab passed, rumbling across a patch of cobblestones; no matter how many times they're paved over, the cars wear the asphalt away, and the ancient stones emerge again, like curious turtles out of black water.

"French Revolution," I said. My voice was slightly breathless.

Jen leaned against me. "Go on."

I smiled—she was getting used to my wandering brain—and pointed at the bumpy surface. "The hoi polloi were pissed off everywhere back in the old days, but the revolution succeeded only in France, because the cobblestones in Paris weren't stuck down very well. An angry mob could take on the king's soldiers just by pulling up the street. Imagine a hundred peasants lobbing those at you."

"Ouch."

"Exactly," I said. "Your fancy uniform, your musket, none of it's worth much in a hail of rocks the size of a fist. But in cities where the cobblestones were stuck down better, the angry mob couldn't do anything. No revolution."

Jen thought for a few seconds, then gave cobblestones the Nod. "So the hoi polloi could get rid of the aristocrats just because of a flaw in the glue, one that was right under their feet."

"Yeah," I said. "All it took was some Innovator to say, 'Yo, let's pick up these cobblestones and throw them.' And that was the end of society."

We left the shade, and I looked back up at the aging building. The scaffolding clung to the front all the way up, six stories of metal pipes and wooden planks. A faded, decades-old advertisement adorned this side, the pattern of the brick showing through the crumbling paint. I could see where another building had once rested against it, nothing left now but a change in color in the bricks.

"Hunter, do you ever feel like there's some problem with the glue these days? Like maybe if anyone figured out what to throw and who to throw it at, everything would fall apart pretty quickly?"

"All the time."

"Me too." We were crossing a worn patch of Hudson Street, and Jen swung a shoe at the top of a cobblestone. It was solidly submerged in sun-baked tar and didn't budge. "So, that's the anti-client's mission, isn't it? Ungluing things? Maybe they've figured out what to throw."

"Maybe." I shaded my eyes with one hand and squinted at the next street sign, then at the numbers. Movable Hype was halfway down the block, in an old and towering iron-frame building. "But more likely they're just throwing everything they can."

"Closed on Saturday," I said, stating what should have been obvious even before we'd bothered to walk over here. No one had answered our buzz.

This was a place of business, and no matter how crazy Futura Garamond's typesetting aesthetic might be, he didn't work on Saturdays in summer.

"Good," said Jen, reaching for the buzzers. This motion gave me a nervous feeling in the bottom of my stomach.

Through the speaker: "Yeah?"

In Jen's fake gruff voice: "Delivery."

Muttered by me: "Not this again."

From the buzzer: *buzz*.

Movable Hype was on the top floor, and the stairs wound upward around the old-style elevator, locked up for the weekend at the bottom of its ten-story cage. Jen soon took a half-floor lead—I could see her red laces flashing through the ironwork surrounding the elevator shaft. She took the stairs like someone who lived in a walk-up. (My parents' building was over the critical six-floor limit, so I was used to riding.)

"Wait up!"

She didn't.

When I arrived on the tenth floor, Jen had already found the door to Movable Hype at the end of one long hall. "Locked."

"Gee, that's a surprise. What are we going to do, break it down?"

"Too strong. But check this out."

She led me around a corner to where a set of windows overlooked a central air shaft. In the old days, rents in New York were based on the number of windows a place had. So landlords invented buildings with hollow centers, creating that famous NYC feature: a window that looked out onto someone else's window about three feet away. Mandy always complained about how Muffin, her cockroach-eating cat, would jump across the gap to other tenants' apartments on hot, open-window days, presumably to see if their cockroaches were any tastier or less cat-shy.

Jen pointed through one of the windows. Across the corner of the air shaft was another window, perpendicular to the one we peered through. I could see a few desks and darkened computers.

"Movable Hype," she said, and unlocked the window.

"Jen . . ."

The window slid up, and she hooked a leg out over the hundred-foot drop.

"Jen!"

She reached toward me. "Hold my hand."

"No way!"

"Would you rather I do this alone?"

"Uh, no." I realized this wasn't an idle threat: she was ready to lean across and try the other window whether I helped or not. I felt a burst of sympathy for Emily. If this was Jen at seventeen, what had she been like at ten?

"Look at it this way. It's only a couple of feet across. If it wasn't for the drop, you wouldn't think twice about it."

"Yes, if it wasn't for the certain-death issue, I wouldn't think twice about it."

She looked down. "Pretty certain, yeah. Which is why you're going to hold my hand." She reached out again, impatiently waving me over.

I sighed and grabbed her wrist with both hands.

"Ow. Too tight."

"Live with it."

Jen just rolled her eyes, then leaned her weight away from me and out over the shaft. Her other hand reached the Movable Hype window easily. Her wrist twisted in my hands as she tugged the window sash upward a few inches; then it stuck.

"Hang on." She shifted her weight on the sill, leaning farther out. I leaned back as if Jen was a rope in a tug-of-war, propping my feet against the wall just below her. She managed to pull the opposite window open another foot.

"Okay, you can let go now."

"Why?"

"So I can go over, silly."

I thought about refusing, just standing there holding her wrist until my hands wore out, keeping her on the sane side of the air shaft. But she would just outwait me. And cutting off the circulation in one of her hands wasn't much of an answer to the certain-death issue.

"Okay, letting go." I straightened, releasing Jen gradually, and she shook out her wrist.

"Ow. But thanks."

"Just be careful."

She smiled again and swung the other leg out. "Duh."

Keeping a white-knuckled grip on the near window with one hand, she slowly slid her weight from the sill, planting one black trainer in the corner of the air shaft. Her other hand reached out and grasped the other sill, then she pulled herself across.

In the seconds when her weight was equidistant between the windows, I felt my stomach flip inside out and then twist once around. I wanted to grab her hand again but knew that my sweat-slick palms were the last thing she needed contact with at this exact moment. Then she was across, both hands on the far sill, her feet scrabbling on the outside wall to push her up through the open window.

The red laces disappeared inside with a muffled crash.

"Jen?"

I leaned out, not looking down at the vertiginous drop.

Her face appeared in the window, all grins.

"Wow. That was cool!"

I took a deep breath, adrenaline still pounding through me. Now that Jen was safely over the air shaft, I realized that I was itching to get across myself. Funny how that happens: a minute ago I'd thought the idea was completely nuts, but once I'd seen an Innovator do it, I was dying to be next in line.

I remembered my resourcefulness in the meteorite room, my mighty escape through the valley of the Poo-Sham flashes. I had no bangs and I was ready for danger.

I hooked one leg out. The air shaft seemed to tug at me, calling me to cross it.

"Uh, Hunter . . ."

"No, I want to get in there too."

"Of course, but—"

"I can make it!"

She nodded. "I'm sure, but I *could* just unlock the door, you know."

I froze, my weight poised evenly atop the sill, one hand clutching the near window in a grip of death, the other reaching out over oblivion. . . .

"Yeah, I guess you could do that."

I pulled myself back in and padded down the hall to the slightly less challenging entrance of Movable Hype. The metal-jacketed door rattled once for every keyhole, then opened.

"You're not going to believe this," Jen said.

TWENTY-SIX

THE WALLS WERE COVERED WITH THEM. PAGES AND PAGES.

They weren't the usual Futura Garamond layouts. For once he had reined himself in, mimicking exactly the pseudo-hip but unthreatening style of a certain magazine for rich young trust-funders.

"Hoi Aristoi," Jen said.

"Sort of." I looked closer. The photographs in the layouts were all from the party, penguins and penguinettes looking drunken and wild-eyed, almost animal in their petty squabbles, overt jealousies, posturings for status. You could read the body language like a neon sign. The crumpled dresses and crooked bow ties were also crystal clear. As the pictures progressed, the whole machine of privilege and power became unglued before your eyes—as pathetic as a cummerbund spattered with Noble Savage. By contrast, the occasional stuffed caribou glimpsed in the background seemed intelligent and sane.

Thousands of printed photos were piled on a long workbench along the wall, the booty of five hundred cameras, an embarrassment of riches. As per Jen's theory, every photo taken on the giveaway cameras had been wirelessly captured by the anti-client.

"Futura must have come back here after the party and worked all night," I said, looking nervously at the entrance to the office. "You suppose he went home to sleep or just out for coffee?"

"He'll probably be back soon," Jen said. "These pages must have already been laid out, just waiting for the photos. Which means they want a quick turnaround."

"Okay," I said, edging toward the door. "Speaking of quick turn-arounds . . ."

"But what's this going to be?" Jen asked. "A fake issue of *Hoi Aristoi* or a real one?"

I shrugged. "It's whatever people decide it is, I guess."

"The cover must be this way."

She followed the wall, counting down the page numbers. I despaired of a hasty exit and went after her. The job was completely professional: Futura Garamond wasn't going for parody; he had created an exact imitation. He had even added real advertisements lifted from the first issue. Of course, the ads were as essential to the magazine as anything else.

At the far end of the office we reached the masthead and cover. The headlines read: *Launch Party Exclusive! Special Subscribers-Only Issue!*

"Issue zero," Jen said, pointing at the upper-right corner of the cover.

"That's what they usually call trial issues of new magazines. But *Hoi Aristoi* already tested their prototype. The free one we got in our gift bags was issue number one."

"So this isn't real."

"No, but it looks real enough," I said. Except for the grotesque photographs, it would have fooled anybody.

"Well, I guess you were right—this isn't blackmail. It's something much weirder. But *what*, exactly?"

"Good question."

We looked around the office. The late-afternoon sun slanted in through the windows, filling the loft with warm light, revealing the inevitable layer of dust on darkened computer screens. High-end printers waited to feed on wide spools of paper, and stacks of big hard drives flickered away in semi-sleep. A few laptops sat around a pile of wireless base stations. No doubt they had captured the launch party photos from the Wi-Fied Poo-Sham cameras.

I found a few issues of Futura Garamond–designed magazines from the past, a mocked-up bottle of Poo-Sham, and a few sketches for the label of Noble Savage rum. So that had been a fake too. I wondered how strong the stuff in the bottles was and if it had been just alcohol or something more. There was nothing to suggest that Movable Hype had any real clients. Garamond was working for the anti-client full time.

"Check this out," Jen said. She was holding a thick, accordion-folded printout. "Names and addresses. Phone numbers, too."

"A mailing list. I wonder if it's *the* mailing list."

Jen looked up at me. "You mean all the *Hoi Aristoi* subscribers?"

I nodded. "See if you can find Hillary Winston-Smith. She's under *W*, not *S*."

Jen flipped to the end of the mailing list. "Yeah. Here she is."

"So it *is* the *Hoi Aristoi* mailing list." I glanced over Jen's shoulder to scan the addresses and confirmed my theory. Every third one was on Fifth Avenue—a few of them actually lacked apartment numbers. Owning an entire house in Manhattan is like having your own airport anywhere else: it means you are *rich*. Hillary Winston-hyphen-Smith's address was no slouch, for that matter: she resided in a certain Upper East Side building famous as a home for movie stars, oil sheiks, and arms dealers.

"They bought the subscriber list," I said.

"So they're going to send out copies to all their victims," Jen said, chuckling. "That's friendly of them."

"And all the wannabe subscribers as well, just to show them what aristocrats are really like. I bet the press gets issues too." I shook my head. "But why? All this money just for a practical joke?"

Jen nodded. "What did you say to me after I pissed off Mandy at the focus group? Messing things up takes talent, right?"

"Yeah." I looked around. "Garamond's got plenty of talent, that's for sure."

"And he's got a plan, too, which I'm starting to figure out. Sort of."

"Please, let me in on it."

She shook her head. "I'm not totally sure yet. But we're getting closer. It would help if we knew who else was behind this." She pointed at the mailing list. "How much would that cost?"

I leafed through the printout, pondering the question. Whether they're about snowboards, pet ferrets, or the latest gadgets, most magazines make more money from selling their subscriber list than they do off newsstand sales. It's big business to know how people perceive themselves, how much they earn, and how they're likely to spend it. A magazine may just be wrapping for advertisements, but it's also a bible for a lifestyle: it tells readers what's going on, what to think about it, and, most importantly, what to buy next. That's why you get a ton of new junk mail every time you subscribe to a magazine—you've pigeonholed yourself as a snowboarder, ferret lover, or gadget buyer.

Advertisers divide humanity into marketing categories, tribes with names like Shotguns and Saddles, Inner City, or Bohemian Mix. Magazine subscriptions are the easiest way to tell who's what. In my hand I was holding a list of high-grade, uncut Blue Bloods. Hot property.

"Very pricey, like the rest of this operation."

"Well, I bet you Movable Hype didn't pay for it."

"Why not? Futura's made decent money over the years."

She nodded. "Sure, he has. But would he want everyone to know he was behind a job like this?" Her gesture took in the pages stretching along the walls. "Something so unoriginal and tame? Even if it's a great practical joke, it's pure imitation."

"Yeah, and also pretty likely to guarantee he never works in the magazine industry again."

"So somebody else paid for it. Someone involved with the anti-client."

I shrugged. "Even if we could find out who paid for the mailing list, wouldn't it just be a front company or something? Like Poo-Sham, Inc.?"

Jen nodded. "Maybe. But whoever's putting up the cash had to pay for the really expensive stuff in those gift bags: hundreds of bottles of Poo-Sham and Noble Savage, not to mention all those wireless cameras. Those aren't things you can just stick on your credit card. There must be some kind of money trail."

"Okay." I looked at the front door of the office, imagining keys jingling at any moment. At least this would get us out of here. "Where do we start?"

She lifted up the mailing list. "With this. Doesn't your friend Hillary work for *Hoi Aristoi?*"

"Hillary doesn't work for them; she just did some PR. And she's not my friend."

"Still, she'd tell you what she knows, wouldn't she?"

"Give me private information about a client? Why would Hillary do that?"

Jen grinned. "Because she's probably dying to find out who turned her head purple."

CHAPTER TWENTY-SEVEN

START WITH A MOLLUSK, WIND UP WITH AN EMPIRE.

Sounds tricky, but the Phoenicians managed it about four thousand years ago. Their tiny sliver of a kingdom was wedged between the Mediterranean Sea and a vast desert: no gold mines, no olive trees, no amber waves of grain anywhere in sight. The only thing the Phoenicians had going for them was a certain species of shellfish, commonly found lying around down at the beach. These shellfish were tasty but had one problem—if you ate too many of them, your teeth turned purple.

Naturally, most people were annoyed by this. They probably said stuff like, "Those shellfish aren't bad, but who wants purple teeth?" and didn't think much more about it.

Then one day an ancient Innovator got this crazy idea. . . .

Okay, imagine you live in Egypt or Greece or Persia back then and you're rich. You've got all the gold, olive oil, and grain you want. But all you ever get to wear is cloth robes that come in the following colors: light beige, medium beige, dark beige. You've seen the Bible movies: everyone's totally decked out in earth tones—that's all they had, that's all they could imagine having.

Then one day along comes a boatload of Phoenicians, and they're selling purple cloth. *Purple!*

Throw that beige wardrobe away!

For a while, purple is *the* thing, the biggest fad since that whole wheel craze. After a lifetime spent wearing sixteen shades of beige, everyone's lining up to buy the cool new cloth. The price is crazy high, partly due to demand and partly because it happens to take about 200,000 shellfish to make one ounce of dye, and pretty soon the Phoenicians are rolling in dough (actually, they're rolling in gold, olive oil, and grain, but you get the picture).

A trading empire is born. And talk about branding: *Phoenicia* is the ancient Greek word for "purple." You are what you sell.

After a while, however, an interesting thing happens. The people in charge decide that purple is too cool for just anyone to wear. First they tax purple cloth; then they pass a law forbidding the hoi polloi to wear purple (as if they could afford it); and finally, they make purple robes the sole property of kings and queens.

Over the centuries this dress code becomes so widespread and so ingrained that even now, four thousand years later, the color purple is still associated with royalty throughout Europe. And all this because an Innovator who lived forty centuries ago figured he could make something cool out of the purple-teeth problem. Not bad.

But why am I telling you all this?

A few days after the *Hoi Aristoi* launch party, as rumors about purple-headed Blue Bloods spread across New York and big chunks of the wealthiest segment of society disappeared to the Hamptons to wait out the dye in royal isolation, some concerned parent had a half-empty bottle of Poo-Sham tested to see what was in it. The shampoo was discovered to contain water, MEA–lauryl sulfate, and awesome concentrations of medically safe, environmentally sound, and righteously staining shellfish dye.

One thing about the anti-client: they knew their history.

◇　◆　◇

Hillary Winston-hyphen-Smith was not receiving visitors.

We were in the lobby of an upper–Fifth Avenue building that was home to sport-star millionaires, software billionaires, and a certain recording artist who goes by only one name. (And come to think of it, that name is royalty-related, and the guy really likes purple. Go figure.) The concierge of the building was wearing a tasteful purple uniform that matched the rich purple upholstery of the chairs in the marble-and-gold-filigreed lobby, proving that things hadn't really changed that much in the last four thousand years.

"Miss Winston-Smith isn't feeling well," the concierge confided.

"Oh, that's terrible," I said. "Uh, have you seen her today, by any chance?"

He shook his head. "She hasn't been down."

"You sure you can't call up for us?" Jen asked.

"Some friends came by earlier, and she said she wouldn't be coming down today." The concierge cleared his throat. "Actually, Miss Winston-Smith said she wouldn't be down this *year*. You know how she gets."

I did. And if Hillary was genuinely suffering from Poo-Sham head, I was quite relieved not to be allowed into her august presence.

"Well, that's too bad . . . ," I started, taking a polite step backward.

Then I heard the beeping of Jen making a call. The concierge and I turned to watch her, both paralyzed by astonishment. I hadn't noticed Jen getting Hillary's phone number from the mailing list, and he'd probably never heard anyone speak to Miss Winston-Smith this way.

"Hillary? This is Jen—you met me two days ago at Mandy's meeting. You better be screening this, because Hunter and I are standing at the front desk of your building, and we have a pretty good idea how to find the counteragent for the shampoo you used this morning. We just need a moment of your time and we may be able to help you with the, uh, purple issue. But we're headed out the door now, so unless you—"

The intercom behind the desk popped to life, and a scratchy and crumpled Hillary voice boomed across the lobby.

"Reginald? Would you send them up, please?"

Reginald blinked in surprise, only belatedly remembering to answer Miss Winston-Smith, and pointed toward the elevators.

"Twentieth floor," he said, his eyes full of admiration.

Hillary was in the garden, a large balcony overlooking Central Park, swaddled in a bathrobe and a towel turban, her skin wrinkly and fingertips puckered from what had evidently been a day of showers and baths, her eyes puffy from crying. Her face, hands, forearms up to the elbow, and the few stray locks of hair that emerged from her turban were all extraordinarily, vibrantly, royally purple.

It was a good look for her. The dye had settled evenly across her skin and looked unexpectedly stunning against her blue eyes. Hillary had achieved her cool status as an eye-candy interviewer for a certain music-video cable channel. Her features were as blue-blooded as her social connections, and although she'd always looked way too commercial for my liking, turning purple had lent her a certain downtown credibility.

"How come you're normal, Hunter?" she said as Jen and I stepped out into the sun. I heard the servant who'd ushered us through the immense, many-floored apartment retreat quickly behind us.

"Normal how?" I asked.

"Not purple!"

I held up my hands, which still bore the stain of my brief exposure to Poo-Sham.

"Wait, that's right. . . ." Her purple brow furrowed, as if she was through a thick hangover to remember the night before. "I asked you about your hands last night."

"Right," I agreed, wondering what her point was.

"Hunter! You already had that crap on your hands when I saw you last night. Why didn't you *warn* me?"

I opened my mouth, then closed it. Good question. I suppose I'd been more worried about joining Mandy in captivity than saving a bunch of Blue Bloods from purple heads. (But frankly, the concept of raising an alarm hadn't crossed my mind.)

"Well, things were kind of complicated last night, and—"

"We were working undercover," Jen said. "Trying to figure out who's behind all this."

"Undercover?" Hillary raised a purple eyebrow. "What the hell are you talking about? Who *are* you, anyway?"

"You met me the other—"

"I *know* where we met, but where did you come from? And why is everything so weird since you showed up?"

Hillary's violet fury brought me up short. Things *had* been odd since I'd known Jen—I'd already noticed that myself once or twice. But in a moment of mental clarity, I realized that this would all be happening far away from my little world if I'd never met her. I never would have gone to the launch party or snuck into Movable Hype. For that matter, if Jen hadn't brought up the missing-black-woman formation at the meeting, Mandy wouldn't have taken us to the abandoned building. Maybe Mandy wouldn't even have gone herself that particular morning and might still be around, running focus groups and taking pictures of guys in berets instead of . . . being gone.

But Hillary's purple features weren't actually Jen's fault. The *Hoi Aristoi* party had been planned for months. Jen wasn't a bad-luck charm making all this stuff happen; she was more like a compass, unerringly guiding me toward the weird. Or something like that.

I decided to work it out later. "Like Jen said, we were working undercover. Mandy disappeared yesterday, and we've been trying to find her."

"Mandy?" Hillary lifted a Bloody Mary from the table beside her lounge chair and emptied it. Hair of the dog. Even dyed purple, Hillary was looking a little green around the gills, probably the result of too much Noble Savage. "What's this got to do with her?"

"We're not quite sure," I said. "In fact, we're completely not sure."

Hillary rolled her eyes. "Gee, Hunter. I'm so thrilled you guys are on the case."

"Like I said, it's complicated. But we think we can track down the people behind Poo-Sham. We just need some information from you."

"But you didn't even . . ." She blinked, and for a moment I thought she was going to cry. I looked away, past exotic plants and potted trees, across the park to the jagged Midtown skyline, looking like broken teeth rising out of a forest.

Hillary sobbed once. "You just walked away from me, Hunter. You must have known it was dye."

"Well, yeah, I guess. But I really didn't have any idea what was going on. I mean, all those flashing lights were freaking me out. . . ."

"Let me ask you one question, Hillary," Jen said. "When you stepped out of the shower and saw yourself, did you immediately sit down and call all your friends to warn them?"

"I——," she started, but her words dissolved into purple bemusement. "Maybe not right away. But that was *this morning*. Hunter knew there was something up last night at the party."

"And your point is . . . ?"

She waved away Jen's question as though it were an annoying mosquito. "You wouldn't think this was so funny if you were purple."

"I don't think it's . . . ," Jen started, then spread her hands. "Well, *aspects* of it are funny."

Hillary groaned. "This has been fun, Hunter. But I think you two are leaving." She stabbed at a wireless intercom next to the empty Bloody Mary glass, and a distant buzzer sounded from within the apartment.

"Listen," I said, "I'm sorry I didn't warn you about the dye, Hillary. But we can find the people who did this to you."

She glared at me. "Too late to help."

"But if we find these guys," Jen said, "we might find the antidote."

The servant returned, hovering at the door to the garden while Hillary's narrowed eyes tried to burn a hole through Jen.

"Antidote?"

Jen shrugged. "Maybe there's a way to wash it off."

"Another Bloody," Hillary commanded, shaking the ice in the empty glass, her gaze still locked on Jen. The servant evaporated.

After a moment of purple calculation she said, "What do you need?"

"To learn the names of everyone who paid for the *Hoi Aristoi* subscriber list," I said.

"The mailing list? Okay, I'll make some calls." She leaned forward, removing the straw from her empty drink and pointing it at me threateningly. "But this time around you better keep me in the loop, Hunter. Or you're going to wake up with something worse than a purple head."

TWENTY-EIGHT

WE WAITED FOR THE CALL DOWNTOWN, BACK AT OUR FAVORITE coffee shop, sitting on our musty couch, shoulders touching. It should have felt wonderful.

"What's bumming you out?"

I looked down at my purple hands. "Hillary being right. I should have told someone about the shampoo last night after I found out it was dye. The whole party was a trap, and we just let everybody walk into it."

Jen leaned her weight into me comfortingly. "Come on. We were too busy not getting caught. And I mean really caught, not dyed purple or photographed behaving badly. Didn't you have to run for your life?"

"Yeah, twice in one day. But I still wish I'd said something to Hillary."

"You feel guilty about Hillary's purple head? News update, Hunter: She'll live. We went to that party to investigate a kidnapping, not rescue a bunch of spoiled rich kids."

I pulled away to get a better look at the smirk just visible on Jen's lips. "You like these guys, don't you?" I said. "The anti-client."

"Well, I wouldn't say I *like* them." She leaned back into the musty couch and sighed. "I think they're probably dangerous, and I'm worried about Mandy. And I definitely don't want to get caught by them."

"But . . . ?"

"But I *do* like their style," she said, then smiled. "Don't you?"

I opened my mouth, then closed it. It was true: the anti-client did have style. They were cool, and they were using cool in a strange new way. I'd spent years studying how Innovators changed the world, and the process was always indirect, suggestive, filtered through cool hunters and Trendsetters and ultimately giant companies while the Innovators remained invisible. As in an epidemic, Patient Zero was always the hardest guy to find. So there was something fascinating about an Innovator taking direct action. The anti-client was shooting advertisements, taking over launch parties, creating their own weird marketing campaign.

I wanted to see what they would do next.

"Maybe," I admitted. "But what do you think they want?"

"In the long run?" Jen sipped some coffee. "I think you were right about the cobblestones."

"The anti-client wants to throw rocks?"

"No. Well, maybe a few, now and then. But I think mostly they want to loosen the mortar, the glue that holds the street down."

I frowned; this line of thinking was bringing on a paka-paka headache. "Could you maybe unmix this metaphor a little?"

Jen took my hand. "You know what glue I mean. The stuff that controls how everyone thinks, how they see the world."

"Advertising?"

"Not just advertising, but the whole system: marketing categories, tribal boundaries, all the formations that people get trapped in. Or locked out of."

I shook my head. "I don't know. Issue zero of *Hoi Aristoi* takes on a pretty easy target. And I mean, what are they saying? Rich, spoiled kids are laughable? Not exactly a revolutionary concept."

"So you're going to tell Hillary Hyphen about what you saw at

Movable Hype? With her connections, she could probably stop the whole thing before it ever hits a printing press."

I laughed. "Hell, no."

"Exactly. Because you want to see it get mailed out. You want to see what happens. Everyone who gets their hands on a copy will devour every page, even the unlucky people in those pictures. Because it's information from outside the system. And we're all starving for it."

"But what good does it do?" I asked.

"Like I said, it loosens the mortar that holds the cobblestones down."

"So they can throw more rocks?"

"No, Hunter. Don't you get it? The anti-client doesn't just want to throw rocks. They want the whole street to come up. They want to make it so *everyone* starts throwing rocks."

A few minutes later a horn sounded outside; a stretch limo waited on the street in the lengthening shadows of early evening. As we approached, a darkened rear window opened a few inches and a purple hand reached out, clutching a single sheet of paper. I felt the cold breath of the car's air-conditioning and glimpsed an even colder stare: a young and purple *hoi aristoi* glaring out at me from the backseat.

He disappeared as the window slid closed. Jen scanned the paper as I watched the car easing into traffic, taking its occupant back to the well-guarded precincts of the Upper East Side.

"Well, this is a no-brainer," Jen announced, handing over our prize.

The short list was on *Hoi Aristoi* stationery, apple-green paper embossed with gold, printed in rich purple ink. It included all the usual suspects: a certain maker of overpriced handbags, a bank in a certain tropical country known for its absence of tax laws, the national committee of a certain political party. But one stood out from among the rest, as inconspicuous as a black widow spider on a piece of Wonder Bread.

"Two-by-Two Productions."

"Sound familiar?" Jen said.

I remembered Hiro's words when he'd recounted the in-line-skating split with Mwadi Wickersham: *Two-by-two or death.*

I had to laugh. "Maybe this *is* all about the wheels."

TWENTY-NINE

WHEN ENGLISH GENTLEMEN WENT HUNTING A LONG TIME AGO, they would occasionally cry at the top of their lungs, "Soho!" (I'm not sure why. Maybe Soho was Tallyho's brother or something like that.) Much later, when some fine hunting grounds near London were paved over to build shops, theaters, and nightclubs, some real-estate genius decided to call this cool new neighborhood "Soho."

Rather later still, a derelict bit of industrial New York just south of Houston Street was being rebuilt with shops, theaters, and nightclubs, and yet another real-estate genius decided to rebrand this cool new neighborhood "SoHo," meaning "South of Houston."

Soon everyone was getting into the act. The folks north of Houston said they lived in "NoHo," lower Broadway went by "LoBro," and the area North Of Where Holland's Entrance Removes Exhausted Suburbanites began to be called, fittingly, NOWHERESville.

So many real-estate geniuses, so little dengue fever.

These days, when young, cool types are hunting for shops, theaters, and nightclubs, they have been known to cry out, "Dumbo!" which stands for Down Under Manhattan Bridge Overpass, a landscape of crumbling factories and industrial vistas that is the last refuge of the truly cool. This week.

Here's how to get there:

We rode the F train to York Street, the cutting edge of Brooklyn. The train was pretty quiet, just the usual coolsters carrying guitar cases and laptops, decorated with tattoos and metal and all coming home from their jobs as designers/writers/artists/fashion designers. I even recognized one of them from our coffee shop, probably one of those guys writing a first novel set in a coffee shop.

Jen and I climbed out of the station and walked up York. To our left, the span of Manhattan Bridge stretched back over the river. For once I didn't have that vague discomfort of not being in Manhattan. Given that the anti-client was made up of renegade cool hunters, it made sense that the hunt was winding up here. Most of the obvious hipsters on the train had gotten off with us, lighting up cigarettes and cell phones as they disappeared down the old streets and into restored industrial buildings. I earnestly hoped that this neighborhood would still be cool when I moved out from my parents' place, but I doubted it. I would probably be letting out a hunting cry of "NewJerZo" by the time I could afford a place of my own.

York Street curled to the west, leading us to Flushing Avenue and past the Brooklyn Navy Yard, the home of Two-by-Two Productions.

I'd seen old pictures of the yard in the Museum of Natural History, during my time among the meteorites. The giant hunk of space iron that had concealed me had spent a few years here about a century ago as people tried to figure out what to do with thirty-four tons of extraterrestrial souvenir. I wondered if it had pulled the compasses of passing ships toward it and if this corner of Brooklyn was one of those mystic spots that had always attracted weird stuff. It was named after a flying elephant, after all.

These days the Brooklyn Navy Yard has no meteorites, no navy, no ships at all. The huge ship-construction buildings have been turned into film studios, offices, and giant open spaces for the companies who create sets for Broadway musicals.

"I wonder why the anti-client needs this much room," Jen said as we walked along.

"Scary question. You could hide anything out here. A fleet of airships, a plague of locusts . . . a suburban house and lawn."

"Jesus. And you think *I'm* wired funny."

We wandered into a security office and asked how to find Two-by-Two Productions. The guard pulled his eyes from his tiny TV and looked us up and down.

"Are they casting again?"

"Uh, yeah."

"Thought they were moving out on Monday."

"That's still the plan," Jen said, nodding. "But they said they wanted to see us right away."

"Okay." He reached for a stack of photocopied maps of the navy yard, scrawled a red *X* on the top one, and handed it over as his eyes drifted back toward the television.

Outside, Jen was incensed. "Casting? I can't believe he thought we looked like actors." (Most Innovators don't like actors, who are, by definition, imitators.)

"I don't know, Jen. You gave a pretty convincing performance in there."

She glared at me.

"Of course," I added, "they could be shooting an ad for the shoe."

"Well, I'd be into that, I guess. But the thought that we came over from central casting . . ." She shivered.

The navy yard was almost empty on a Saturday, the open spaces dizzying after the narrow streets of Manhattan. We walked under giant arches of rusted metal speckled with flaking paint, crossed paved-over railroad tracks that raised long ripples in the asphalt. We wandered between ancient, empty factories and prefab metal hangars lined with the growling butts of air conditioners.

"Here it is," I said.

The name Two-by-Two Productions was stenciled on a huge sliding door set into an old brick building you could have hidden a battleship in.

I felt my nerves starting to tingle: this was the moment where Jen would take over, leading us through some roundabout, dangerous, and probably illegal means of entry.

But there was no point resisting fate.

"So how do we get in?" I asked.

"Maybe this way?" Jen pulled at the huge handle of the door, and it slid open. "Yeah, that worked."

"But that means . . ."

Jen nodded and held up her Wi-Fi bracelet, which sparkled. She fingernailed a tiny switch to douse its light and whispered, "It means that they're here, probably packing up for the move. Better be quiet."

Inside, it was pitch black.

We crept among formless shapes, engulfed in a lightless silence. Jen bumped into something that scraped angrily against the concrete floor. We both froze until the echo trailed away, suggesting a vast space around us.

As my eyes grew accustomed to the darkness, the cluster of objects around me felt somehow familiar, as if I had visited this place before. I forced my eyes to resolve shapes from the darkness. We were passing through a small group of tables, a few overturned chairs resting on them.

I reached out and brought Jen to a halt with a tug.

"What does this look like to you?" I whispered.

"I don't know. A closed restaurant?"

"Or a set that's supposed to look like a restaurant. Sort of like the one in the Poo-Sham ad." I ran my fingers across one of the chairs, trying to recall the advertisement. "Where the guy orders lack of ram."

She looked around. "Are you sure?"

"No." I squinted into the darkness, letting shapes form before my eyes. "Are those old theater seats over there?

"Why would they be?"

"There was a scene in a theater. Where the usher gets all tongue-tied."

"Why would they build a theater on a sound stage?" Jen shook her head. "We're in New York, land of theaters, and they couldn't go on location?"

"Huh." I crossed to the group of seats. It was only five or so rows, maybe ten seats across, with a red velvet curtain hanging as a backdrop. But Jen was right. It seemed like a crazy expense in a city full of real theaters, not to mention restaurants. "Maybe they wanted a controlled situation. Absolute secrecy."

"Maybe they're just nuts," Jen said.

"That's one thing I'm pretty sure—"

"*Shhh.*" Jen stood stock-still in the darkness. She cocked her head and pointed to our left.

I heard a voice echoing across the cavernous space.

"Is that who I think it is?" Jen whispered.

I peered through the gloom toward the sound, listening intently. The barest sliver of light glimmered from the other side of the cavernous studio, a band of illumination creeping from under a door, wavering along its length as someone walked past on the other side. The voice continued, the words consumed by the distance but the strident tone utterly familiar.

It was Mandy Jenkins, sounding very annoyed.

THIRTY

I LOWERED MY VOICE BELOW A WHISPER, JUST BREATH: "KEEP QUIET."

Among the shadowy, jumbled shapes, quiet meant slow. We moved like deep-sea divers, taking slow-motion steps, waving our hands in front of us in the darkness. As we grew nearer, eyes still adjusting, the glow from under the door seemed to grow brighter. The texture of the concrete floor became clearer, its pitted surface lit by the sidelong light like craters on the moon.

Gradually I began to make out that there were other doors along this wall of the studio. Most were dark, but a few showed glints of light under them. More sounds came dully through the wall, grunts and scrapes, the movement of heavy objects across the rough floor. A few metal ladders disappeared up into darkness above us, where a catwalk wound its way around the outside of the studio, accessing a steel framework hung with movie lights and sound equipment.

The door we'd first spotted stood out, the light around its edges glowing fiercely, and I imagined a blinding interrogation lamp pointed at Mandy's face across a bare table.

A sentence formed out of the muffled hum of her voice. "I think you've got this all wrong!"

The reply was too quiet and steady for me make out any words, but it sounded coolly threatening.

The scrape of a chair came from behind the door, then footsteps.

Jen threw herself behind some huge piece of equipment, waving frantically for me to follow. The sliver of light grew darker as someone approached.

I took a few panicked, silent steps to join Jen, crouching beside her just as the door opened, spilling an arc of light across the huge studio. Cowboy boots and red-and-white client shoes swept across my view—NASCAR Man (also known as Futura Garamond) escorting Mandy across the gray concrete expanse.

Darkness wrapped itself around them as the door swung closed, but then illumination poured from overhead, a row of work lights popping on. Jen pulled me farther back behind our hulking piece of equipment just as Futura Garamond looked our way, his hand still on the switch.

I swallowed, pressed hard against Jen, my heart beating frantically. Had he heard my footsteps? Seen us?

"Hello?" he called.

We stayed frozen until he shook his head and guided Mandy to another door a dozen yards away, pulling it open. She went in alone, and Garamond let it swing closed behind her with a *click*.

"I'll be back," he said through the door, then turned and disappeared up one of the ladders, cowboy boots clanking on metal. Peering upward through the catwalk, we watched him clomp right over our heads. Then his footsteps faded.

Jen and I stayed still for a moment, still clinging to each other. Was he still up there, looking down? Waiting for us to emerge? Or did the catwalk lead off into some other part of the building?

After long seconds of waiting Jen said, "Come on."

We crept toward the door through which Mandy had disappeared, me looking up at the dangling work lights. I felt naked in the light, but

Garamond, wherever he was, might notice if they clicked off again.

When we got to the door, Jen reached out and softly grasped the knob, turning it as carefully as a safecracker.

She shook her head. Locked.

I put my ear to the cold metal and heard nothing. This must be where they kept Mandy between interrogations. What were they trying to do? Learn the client's marketing secrets? Dig up dirt on their overseas operations? Find out more about *me?*

Whatever the anti-client wanted from Mandy, now was the time to rescue her. And quickly. Futura Garamond had said he was coming back.

Jen mimed a knock on the door, a questioning look on her face.

I quickly shook my head. The last thing we needed was Mandy calling out, asking who we were. Her sharp voice was famous for its ability to get the attention of unruly focus groups.

I made a punching gesture at the door, and Jen nodded agreement. We were going to have to break it down.

Unfortunately, we hadn't remembered to bring a battering ram. The door looked formidable, its metal painted industrial gray. And once the first blow rang out, we were going to have company pretty soon. We would have to crash through, drag Mandy out, and make a run for the other end of the studio.

I looked around for something to hit the door with and spotted a fire extinguisher hanging in a corner.

Jen stepped in front of me, shaking her head. She pointed back to where we'd hidden.

In the work lights I could clearly see the piece of equipment we had crouched behind. It was a camera dolly, a heavy, four-wheeled cart used for filming traveling shots. Attached to its front was a heavy, cranclike arm for holding the camera.

I smiled. We did have a battering ram.

We stole quickly back to the dolly and gave it a tentative shove. It glided forward easily on rubber tires designed to provide the camera with a smooth, silent ride.

Jen and I grinned at each other. Perfect.

We lined it up with the door, aiming the camera crane dead center.

"One . . . two . . . three . . . ," Jen mouthed, and we leaned our weight against the dolly. Engineered to roll fast, it built speed quickly and quietly moved across the smooth floor.

About five seconds from collision the door opened.

Mandy was standing there, a puzzled look on her face, the small room glaringly white behind her. I skidded to a halt, but our battering ram pulled itself from my grasp, rolling unstoppably ahead.

"W-What the . . . ," Mandy stammered as the dolly hurtled toward her; then, at the last instant, she did the sensible thing and slammed the door shut.

The dolly struck with a bright metal crunch, the sound of a car hitting a garbage can at full speed echoing through the vast space. The door crumpled inward, closing around the dolly's camera crane like a stomach around a fist.

"Mandy!" I cried, leaping forward.

Jen and I pulled the dolly back frantically, and the door swung outward, then tumbled from its hinges, crashing to the floor.

Mandy was standing inside the little room, looking down at us from her perch. I realized she'd jumped up onto a toilet to escape the rampaging dolly—she was in a bathroom. The sounds of flushing noises came from the imperturbable plumbing.

"Are you okay?" I shouted.

"Hunter? What the hell are you—?"

"No time!" I cried, and pulled her down. Jen was already headed back across the studio floor, out of the pool of work lights and into the darkness. I dragged a very stunned Mandy after me, bruising my shins against shadowy obstacles as we charged for the big sliding stage door.

The sounds of confusion came from behind me, doors swinging open and light spilling into the studio. If only we could make it back to the security guard at the front entrance or even out into the sunlight . . .

"Hunter!" Mandy screamed, a dead weight behind me.

"Just run!" I yelled, trying to yank her forward, but she planted her heels and pulled me to a stop.

I spun and faced her.

"What are you *doing?*" she cried.

"Rescuing you!"

She looked at me for an endless second, then sighed and shook her head. "Oh, Hunter, you are so yesterday."

Then the world exploded, buzzing and powerful banks of film lights hitting us from every direction.

"Oh, shit," I heard Jen say.

I covered my eyes against the blaze of color, completely blind. Footsteps and the sound of metal skate wheels closed around us.

Oh, shit, was right.

THIRTY-ONE

A COMMANDING VOICE CAME FROM BEHIND THE BLINDING WALL of light.

"If it isn't Hunter Braque, skinny white boy looking like his mother didn't have time to dress him."

Even blinded and terrified, I flinched at this unfair fashion analysis. I might be wearing gray cords and a dried-chewing-gum-colored shirt, but I was going for social invisibility.

"I *am* undercover, you know," I protested.

"Yeah, you look it," a deeper voice called from the opposite direction—the big bald guy.

"And who have we here?" the first voice said.

I heard the rumble of skates on the concrete floor. I agonizingly pried my lids apart and saw Mwadi Wickersham gliding gracefully out of the retina-searing glare. I glimpsed more figures surrounding us, covering every escape route. The trucker cap and cowboy boots of Futura Garamond strolled out of the blinding wall of light. He stared at Jen's feet.

"Yo, look, she's got the laces," he said. A murmur of recognition passed through our captors.

"So she does," Mwadi Wickersham said, dark glasses peering down from her skate-enhanced height. "Did you come up with those yourself, honey?"

Jen squinted back at her. "Yeah. What do you mean, *the* laces?"

"Mandy had a picture on her. We've all been talking about them." Mwadi nodded, an imperious queen pleased with her subject. "Nice work."

"Uh, thanks."

"Let us go!" I demanded, if high-pitched noises can be construed as demanding.

Mwadi Wickersham turned toward me and said, "Not until we get a deal signed."

I turned toward Mandy, who was giving me the glare she reserves for people who perpetually insist that clam diggers are coming back.

"W-Wait," I stammered. "What deal?"

"The biggest deal of my career, Hunter." She sighed. "Do you think maybe you could *not* screw it up?"

We sat at one of the tables in the fake restaurant: Jen and me, Mwadi Wickersham, Mandy, and Futura Garamond. A few more henchmen stood around, half visible behind the bright banks of movie lights. I caught the flash of Future Sarcastic Woman's silver hair and the silhouette of the big bald guy, their alert poses suggesting that departure was not an option. From our island of light, the sound stage seemed to extend for miles in every direction, lending an echoey grandeur to our words.

"So you didn't get kidnapped?" I asked Mandy for the third time.

"Well . . . at first, I guess." She looked at Mwadi Wickersham for help with the question.

Wickersham removed her dark glasses, and I blinked. Her eyes were as green as Jen's but more piercing, narrowed to slits in the bright movie lights. She wore a white wife beater and faded, brandless jeans with a wide black belt, a fake gold chain around her neck: banji-butch street kid, circa mid-break-dance era. In winter you'd add a leather jacket. I knew from cool-hunting history that if you'd grown up in the Bronx in the 1980s, the uniform was practically Logo Exile.

She placed the glasses on the table, in no hurry to answer, possessed of that unquestionable authority achieved by being from an older generation but still totally cool.

"We decided to make a deal."

"You made a bargain with the client?" Jen asked, appalled.

"Sure. The element of surprise was blown anyway. And they wanted them."

"That we did," Mandy said.

"Wait," I asked. "You wanted what?"

"You sold out," Jen said to Wickersham.

I felt like I was reading subtitles that didn't match the dialog. "Huh?"

"It wasn't supposed to work out this way," Wickersham said darkly, the rumble of her skates ominous under the table as her feet slid restlessly back and forth. "We worked on those shoes for two years, getting them just right. We wanted to put them on the street with the sinister swooshes. But certain people in our organization thought they were *too* cool. A theory was proposed that we'd be making the client hip again by association."

"Kind of like a Tony Bennett self-parody thing," Jen said.

I found myself nodding. Some of this was becoming clear. "When we first saw the shoes, we weren't even sure whether they were bootlegs or the client being self-reflexive. So you got nervous, thinking the shoes might backfire?"

"I didn't get nervous," said Wickersham, in a tone that suggested she

never got nervous. "But certain people did, and they acted on their own."
She shrugged. "This is what I get for working with anarchists."

"They called the police?" Jen asked.

"Someone called the client," Mandy said. "Reported a shipment of
bootlegs. Before the boardroom suits called in the cops, they sent a rep
down to check out the shoes, a guy called Greg Harper."

"Your boss," I supplied. "And when he saw them, he must have realized he was looking at bootlegs that were better than the original."

Mandy chuckled. "And a suit like him didn't know how to cope with
that. So he called in street-level expertise, telling me to deal with it."

"And you called in me and Jen," I said.

Futura Garamond spoke up, his trucker cap bobbing. (The logo on it
was the classic naked-girl silhouette found on the mud flaps of eighteen-
wheelers, which was daringly last year of him, I thought.) "By this time,
we'd realized what had happened. So we decided to move the shoes out of
town until the heat was off. But Mandy showed while we were setting up
the move. Certain people panicked." He and Wickersham cast disappointed looks at the big bald guy.

Who shrugged. "Had to improvise, didn't I? Left the shoes, brought in
Mandy. Worked out all right."

"So you *did* kidnap her," Jen said.

"Like I said, I improvised."

I turned to Mandy. "But then you wound up negotiating with them?"
My tone was incredulous, but frankly, cutting a deal with her own kid-
nappers sounded like the Mandy I knew and loved. I could imagine her
tapping her clipboard, ticking off contractual issues one by one.

"A sharp operator, Ms. Wilkins," Wickersham admitted, giving Mandy
the Nod. "She realized that we wanted to ditch the shoes and the client
wanted to buy them. And she offered a good price."

"Just a couple more points and we can wind this deal up." Mandy looked at her watch. "We'd be done by now if you two kids hadn't shown up in rescue mode."

"Yeah, sorry," I said. A scorecard flashed in my head—Amateur Detectives: Still Zero.

"But how could you *sell* them?" Jen pleaded with Wickersham. "They'll go straight into the outlet malls!"

The older woman spread her arms helplessly. "Anarchy's a cash business, girl. The *Hoi Aristoi* operation wound up with some major cost overruns."

Jen nodded slowly, and her expression changed. "So how did that work?" She leaned forward, eyes widening like a Japanese ten-year-old's. "The paka-paka thing, I mean. Have you really figured out how to rewire people?"

Mwadi Wickersham laughed. "Hold on to your skates, girl. I *like* you, but we just met. And I *might* not even know what you're talking about."

Jen smiled sheepishly, her smile luminous from the praise.

Until Mwadi continued: "The question is, what to do with you?"

I shared a sidelong glance with Jen. That question had been on my mind as well.

"Uh, I'm sure the client wants you to let us go," I said, glancing over at Mandy.

She stared back at me silently, still annoyed, her fingers drumming on the table. I swallowed dryly, remembering the client's record on child labor. . . .

Mwadi cleared her throat. "Our deal's pretty much sewn up, and there was no mention of Hunter Braque in the contract. Or you, sweetie. What's your name, anyway?"

"Jen James."

In a weird and off-the-subject flash, it occurred to me that I hadn't known Jen's last name until that moment. As I've said, things were moving quickly.

"Well, Jen James, we might have work for you two."

"Work?" I said.

Mwadi nodded. "We've got other irons in the fire, lots of plans, and now we've got the cash to get them moving. You both know the territory. If you didn't, you never would have made it all the way here."

"What territory?" I asked. I wasn't even sure what planet we were on.

Mwadi rose from the chair to her full two-by-two-wheeled height. She spun around once, reminding me of the ever-rotating Hiro but saturated with grace and power rather than Hiro's nervous energy. She began to skate in slow circuits around the table, frictionless as a swan with a tail-wind, weaving the client's fantasy world (her own weird version) into existence from the multicolored threads of movies lights.

"You know the cool pyramid, don't you, Hunter?"

"Sure." I drew it in the air with two fingers. "Innovators at the top, under them the Trendsetters, then Early Adopters. Consumers at the very bottom, with Laggards scattered around the base, sort of like leftover construction materials."

"Laggards?" She narrowed her eyes at me as she halted, old-school metal wheels scraping the concrete floor like fingernails. "I prefer the term *Classicists*. Rock Steady Crew, still break dancing after twenty-five years? On the cardboard every day, whether breaking's in style or out? They're not Laggards."

"Okay," I agreed. "Rock Steady are Classicists. But guys wearing tucked-in Kiss T-shirts are Laggards."

A grin flashed across her features. "I can live with that." She resumed her fluid circling. "But the pyramid's in trouble. You know that."

"I do?"

"Because of cool hunters," Jen cut in. "And market research, focus groups, and all that crap. They squeeze the life out of everything."

Mandy spread her hands. "Hey, sitting right here!"

"That's the score, though," Wickersham said. "Hunter, your girlfriend knows what she's talking about. The ancient pyramid has sprouted mailing lists and databases. The sides are too slippery now, so nothing sticks anymore. The cool hits the mall before it has time to digest."

And of course, all my brain had processed from this last metaphorical hash was that someone who was not my parents had referred to Jen as my girlfriend. Pathetic.

As a result all I managed was, "Yeah," all soulfully.

"I thought you had it figured out," Wickersham continued, nodding. "While waiting for you to find us, we read most of your old cool blog and got the scoop from a bunch of your friends. We have some of the best social engineers in the history of hacking working for us." She nodded at Future Woman, then turned back to me. "We know you cold, Hunter, and we think that you realize something's wrong with the pyramid. You've known it since you were thirteen."

I felt that lump, the one from my first year in school here. The cobblestone in my stomach. "Yeah, I guess."

"So the pyramid needs some reconstruction work; a new level in the hierarchy needs to be innovated," she said, green eyes flashing in the movie lights. "Something to slow things down again. To trip things up. How well do you know the first heroes, Hunter?"

My knowledge of history includes many obscure details but few big pictures. "First heroes?"

"The first Innovators invented myth," Wickersham said, "before religion got turned into mall metal for Consumers. In those old stories the first heroes were tricksters, coyotes, and hustlers. Their job was to jam nature, mess up the wind and stars. They messed with the gods, remixing the world with chaos."

She slid to a halt.

"So we're taking a page out of the old books, adding Jammers to the pyramid."

"Jammers." Jen's eyes widened. "The opposite of cool hunters."

Mwadi smiled. "Right. We don't help innovations move down the pyramid; we mystify the flow. We market confusion, jam the ads until the Consumers don't know what's real and what's a joke."

"Loosening the glue," I said softly. The floor seemed to rumble beneath my feet. In fact, the floor *was* rumbling.

A wash of red light fell across us, the giant studio door sliding open to let in the last rays of the descending sun.

Outlined against the bloody sky were about a dozen figures. I recognized the one in front: he was the would-be writer from the coffee shop, the one who'd ridden with us on the train into Dumbo. He'd been following us.

The other figures were carrying baseball bats, and their heads and hands were purple.

The *hoi aristoi* had arrived, and they were pissed.

THIRTY-TWO

MWADI WICKERSHAM WAS CHUCKLING.

"Damn, look at those heads. That stuff worked *too* good."

"Run?" Futura asked.

Her broad shoulders shrugged. "Looks like it. You take Mandy, I'll grab these two. See you at the factory. Lights!"

Seconds later the long banks of movie lights all switched off, and once again I couldn't see a thing.

"Come with me, kids." A strong hand grabbed my arm, lifting me to my feet. Then I was running, following the sound of roller skates on concrete, in the wake of an unstoppable force that brushed aside invisible obstacles. From behind us came shouts and crashes as our pursuers stumbled through the hodgepodge of movie sets and lighting. The Jammers were barely visible—a swift, silent horde marked by bobbing flashlights in the dark.

I heard Jen's breath next to me, reached out to feel for her hand. We steadied ourselves against each other as we were led around a sharp turn, then pushed up a ladder, Wickersham's skates clanking on metal rungs behind us. We stormed along the catwalk, then through a door high in the wall. A long hallway opened up before us, dimly lit by a row of dirty skylights, leading to a window red with sunset.

Mwadi zoomed around us, shot ahead on her wheels, and had the security gate open before we caught up. She pulled herself out onto the fire escape, and Jen and I followed. Our combined weight tipped the ancient metal stairs into motion, Mwadi clunking down them as they swung to ground level on a wailing, rusty hinge.

Hitting asphalt, she skated furiously around the corner. Jen and I looked at each other.

"Maybe we should escape now," I said.

"We *are* escaping."

"No, I mean escape the anti-client."

"They're called Jammers, Hunter. Weren't you listening? And we don't have to escape; they want us to work for them."

"What if we don't want to?"

"As if."

Jen turned and dashed after Wickersham. I couldn't do much but follow.

Around the corner Mwadi was zooming up a handicapped ramp to the sliding door—we had circled back around to the sound-stage entrance. She rolled it shut, closed the massive padlock hasp, and jammed her flashlight into it, leaving the *hoi aristoi* trapped in darkness.

"Lucky all that stuff's rented," she said, rumbling back down the ramp. She looked at an empty limo waiting by the door. The driver must have been inside the building with his employer. "Either of you know how to drive?"

"No."

"No."

She shook her head. "Damn city kids. I can hot-wire, but I *hate* driving with skates on."

But Jen was already opening the driver's-side door. "It's okay, I've played tons of . . ." She mentioned a certain video-game franchise with the same name as the crime we were about to commit.

"Good enough for me," Wickersham said.

Already outvoted, I got in.

In 2003 a University of Rochester study revealed that kids who play mega-hours of video games have superior hand-to-eye coordination and faster reflex time. Parents and educators were shocked, appalled, disbelieving.

Every teenager I know was like, *"Duh."*

Jen took us through the empty streets of the Brooklyn Navy Yard fast and furious, leaving streaks of rubber on the hot summer asphalt. She slowed down only when we passed through the open gates and turned onto Flushing, keeping it legal.

I turned to look out the back window. There were no signs of pursuit.

"We're cool."

"What about everyone else?" Jen asked.

"They'll be fine," Wickersham said. "Practice makes perfect."

I had to ask. "You *practice* running away?"

"We knew we'd make enemies. Other organizations have fire drills; we have oh-shit-someone-found-our-ass drills. Now, a question for you two: *why* did someone find us?"

There was an uncomfortable silence.

"Well, you see, when we were tracking you down, we enlisted some help from an acquaintance of mine"—I cleared my throat—"of the purple-headed persuasion. And it appears that she called all her friends, and they called their friends, and someone had us followed."

"That's what I figured." Mwadi shook her head. "And I thought you kids were so damn clever."

"It's my fault," Jen said.

"Not any more than mine," I protested.

Jen's knuckles turned white on the wheel as she grimly followed

Flushing Avenue. "I was the one who told Hillary what we were doing."

"That was just to get her to help," I said. "You didn't plan on telling her what we found out, did you?"

"Of course not. But it was me who spilled the beans. It didn't even occur to me that Hillary might be playing us."

"Take this left," Wickersham said. "And shut up a second."

She made a call, speaking quickly and softly into a cell phone, guiding Jen with gestures. I wondered what was being arranged for us at the other end of this trip now that we were in disgrace.

But part of me felt at peace: finally we had answers. Things had fallen into place, not far from our theories and paka-paka revelations: renegade cool hunters, a charismatic Innovator, a movement that wanted to rock the world. Maybe Jen and I really did know the territory.

It was nice to discover that sometimes the useless facts in my brain had some relevance, that my fantasy world matched up, at least occasionally, with the real one. That all my time spent reading the signals around me hadn't been completely wasted.

Maybe the signs had been around even before Mandy disappeared, as obvious as the stones in the street. People pushing back from being force-fed, ready to rebel; maybe Innovators only channel something that's already there. Maybe the Jammers had to happen.

And whatever else went down, at least Mandy was okay.

I leaned back and closed my eyes, exhausted. There was nothing more to do but wait for the car to get where it was going.

"That way." Mwadi Wickersham flicked her phone closed.

Jen turned, easing us down an alley, the sides of the car scraping stacks of garbage bags. We pulled into a bare courtyard, surrounded on every side by derelict buildings, their black windows watching us like empty eyes. A rental truck was already there, the one we'd spotted on Lispenard Street the day before.

Two figures were tossing shoe boxes from it into an unruly pile. My eyes caught the flicker of reflective panels as shoes tumbled out onto the dirt.

A third person stood next to the growing pile.

She was pouring gasoline onto it.

"No," I whispered.

The limo came to a crunching halt, a bottle popping under one tire. Mwadi leapt out, her wheels gliding across the rubbish-strewn courtyard like it was a hardwood rink.

Jen and I ran to the edge of the pile.

"What are you doing?"

"Getting rid of these, as per our agreement with the client," Wickersham said. "They'll get the prototypes and the specs. The last thing they want is the originals showing up on the street."

"You're *burning* them?" I cried. "They should be in a museum!"

She nodded sadly. "You got that right. But thanks to you two, our security's been compromised. We got to do this quick and dirty."

A match went down onto the pile, and the smell of burning gasoline rushed at us.

"No!" I cried.

Then a wave of heat forced us back, fire spreading across the pile like the sweep of a hand. Shoe-box lids popped off, carried up by the super-heated air, revealing beautiful forms inside. The elegant lines warped and twisted, reflective panels glittering for a few seconds in the blaze before they blackened. The smell of burning plastic and canvas followed, forcing acid tears from my eyes.

Jen tried to shout something but only managed to cough into a clenched fist.

The pyre turned greedy, sucking the air around us into itself. Bits of paper rolled past my feet, drawn toward the blaze by the column of smoke climbing out of the courtyard. Sickeningly, I realized that the thick, black cloud overhead *was* the shoes, transmuted from something beautiful and original into shapeless smoke. I was breathing the dream shoes into my lungs, choking on them.

Mwadi Wickersham shouted orders into her cell phone as the last few boxes were thrown onto the fire before my eyes. I was forced back farther by the heat, helpless to prevent the conflagration. The shoes were going, going . . . gone.

THIRTY-THREE

THEY LEFT US THERE.

"Wish we could work together, but you two are a risky proposition," Mwadi said, pulling herself up into the open maw of the truck.

"We didn't mean to lead them to you." Jen's face was blackened by smoke, streaked by tears. "We were just playing them for information."

"They wound up playing you."

"We'll be more careful next time, I swear."

Wickersham nodded. "You better be careful. The purple heads will be keeping their eyes on you. You're their only link to us. And that makes you useless for future operations."

"But we know the territory, like you said."

"Exactly, and the purple heads know you do. If you keep looking for us, you'll bring them straight to my doorstep."

"But—"

"Just forget we exist, Jen James. Pretend this never happened." She smiled. "If you're good, I'll put you on our mailing list."

Mwadi stamped her skate once against the metal bed of the truck, a sovereign, final sound, and it jerked forward, rumbling in a slow circle around the blackened pile, then out of the courtyard and down the alley.

Jen followed for a few steps, as if to plead her case again, but didn't say anything. She stood silent until the sound of the truck had faded to nothing.

When it was gone, she turned and faced the pile.

"There must be something left."

"What?"

"Pieces, clues." She strode forward to the blackened edge, teeth gritted, her feet kicking ash into the air. "Maybe we can find a sample of the canvas, or an eyelet, or one of those laces."

I almost smiled. With everything in ashes, Jen had returned to her roots: shoelaces.

She dropped to her knees in the smoking pyre, pushing her hands through the ruin, face averted from the heat still coming off the smoking plastic.

"Jen . . ."

"We might even find a whole shoe in here. When houses burn down, they always find weird stuff the fire didn't—" She lost the rest of her words, coughing from the smoke and ash she'd raised. Her hands went to her face, leaving solid black streaks on her cheeks. She gained control of her breathing, then spat out something black.

"Jen, are you crazy?"

She looked up at me, clearly wondering why I wasn't down there with her.

"What are you doing?" I asked.

"What does it look like I'm doing? I'm looking for the damn shoes, Hunter. That's what we've been doing all along!"

I shook my head. "I was looking for Mandy."

She spread her blackened hands. "Well, she turned out to be fine. She's probably up for a promotion. You want to give up now? Just because Mwadi Wickersham tells us to?"

I sighed and walked into the pile, feeling the warmth of the ashes through the soles of my shoes. The sun had gone down, and the remaining light in the courtyard came from the still-glowing core of the fire. I knelt next to Jen.

"Give what up?"

"Looking."

"For what? The shoes are gone."

She shook her head, as hard and angry as a twelve-year-old forced to move to New Jersey. Like the answer couldn't be expressed in words, and only an idiot would think it could. She was looking for lost cool, the hardest thing to find.

I spoke softly. "Jen, maybe it's better this way."

"Better?"

"I mean, do you really want to work for those guys? Carrying out the grand plans of the Jammers? Spending every minute of your life thinking you've got to change the world?"

She glared at me, eyes flashing. "Yeah, that's exactly what I want."

"Really?"

"That's what I've always wanted." She dug into the ash again, raising a black haze that settled over us, forcing me to turn away, eyes shut. "I mean, what do you want to do, Hunter? Go back to watching advertisements for money? Hang out in focus groups and debate whether leg warmers are coming back? Poach the latest shoelaces? Just *watch* instead of making something happen?"

"I don't just watch."

"No, you take pictures and sell them, theorize and read a lot. But you don't *do* anything."

My eyes opened wide.

"I don't do anything?" I sure felt like I'd been doing things, at least for the last two days. Since I'd met Jen.

"No, you don't. You watch. You analyze. You follow. That's the part of the pyramid you like the best: the outside, looking in. But you're afraid to change anything."

I swallowed, the taste of smoke in my mouth like burned toast. No denials came to my lips because frankly, she was right. I'd followed her every step of the way here. Whenever I would have given up, she'd provided the next step. Just as cool hunters have always done, I'd latched onto Jen's initiative, her dogged pursuit of the weird and terrifying.

And in the end, I hadn't even managed the one thing I *am* good at: watching. I hadn't noticed us being followed and had let Jen be used by a bunch of stupid purple heads, leaving her with nothing but ashes.

I remembered sending the picture of her laces to Mandy—selling Jen out the very first time I'd met her. I was nothing but a fraud. As I'd found out from the moment we'd left Minnesota, there wasn't anything cool about me.

I didn't belong with the Jammers or deserve to be with Jen.

"Okay. I'll get out of your way." I stood up.

"Hunter . . ."

"No, I *really* want to get out of your way." I'd never heard my voice so harsh or felt the lump in my stomach so hard.

I walked away, and even before I reached the alley, I heard her back at work, picking through the pile.

THIRTY-FOUR CHAPTER

"DID YOU WASH YOUR HANDS?"

"Yes, I washed my hands."

My father looked up at me, for once finding my tone more disturbing than this morning's terrifying graph.

"Oh, sorry. Of course you did."

Victory. If only I could have smiled. After so many years of trying, I had finally managed exactly the right robotic voice. Toneless, soulless, empty. I knew Dad would never ask me again if I'd washed my hands.

My anger at Jen, and at myself, had faded on the way home the night before, turning to something hard and cold by the time I'd gone to bed. This morning I was a dead thing.

Mom poured me coffee silently.

A solid minute later my father asked, "Long weekend?"

"Very."

"Still love your hair like that," Mom said, her voice tipping up at the end, as though she were asking a question.

"Thanks."

"And those hands don't look as purple today."

"I wouldn't go that far." Under the harsh light of my bathroom mirror, I could see that the dye had faded only a tiny bit. At the current rate of decay, I might be graduating college with non-purple hands.

"Tell us what's wrong, Hunter?" Mom asked.

I sighed. They'd probably already guessed, and I do tell them most things, sooner or later. Might as well get it over with.

"Jen."

"Oh, I'm so sorry, Hunter."

"That was fast," Dad added, bringing his brilliant empirical mind to the matter.

"Yeah, I guess it was." I'd met Jen Thursday afternoon. It was what? Sunday morning?

Mom put her hand on mine. "You want to talk about what happened?"

I shrugged, moved my face around, tried out different sentences in my head, and finally said, "She saw through me."

"Saw through you?"

"Yeah. Straight through." I could still feel the hole her gaze had left. "Remember when we moved here? When I lost all my friends?" My confidence, my cool.

"Of course. That was really hard on you."

"I'm sure it was hard on you guys too. But the thing is, I don't think I ever got over it. It's like I've been a wimp since then. And Jen figured me out—I'm too lame to hang with her."

"Lame?" Dad asked.

I found a better word: "Afraid."

"Afraid? Don't be silly, Hunter." Mom shook her head at a forkful of eggs. "This is probably something you two can work out."

"And if you can't," Dad chimed in, "at least you haven't wasted much time on her."

Mom did a minor coffee spit at this, but I managed to say the mature thing: "Thank you both for trying to make me feel better. But please stop now."

They stopped. And went back to saying and doing the usual, predictable things. Eating breakfast with the parents is always calming: they follow immutable patterns in that married-couple way, as if things have always been and will always be the same. They aren't Innovators. Not at the breakfast table. For one hour every morning they are Classicists of the best kind, my own Rock Steady Crew.

But after I finished and went back into my room, there wasn't much to do but sit on the bed, wishing I still had my bangs to hide behind.

The tiny teams of bottle jerseys were mocking me from their shelves, so I began a little project. I took the jerseys off the empty water bottles one by one, entering the vital statistics of each into eBay, then placing each jersey underneath its own book full of obscure and useless facts, flattening them for shipment.

It was sad to break up the carefully assembled teams, but every general manager has to go into rebuilding mode every few years, sending away the familiar players and starting over with the low draft picks that losers are guaranteed. Plus if the auction gods were good to me, I might have the minimum payment for my next credit-card bill by the time it arrived.

When my phone rang, I closed my eyes and took a breath. *It's not her,* I repeated silently a few times, then forced myself to look at the caller ID.

shugrrl. Mandy.

I should have been glad that she was calling, that she had escaped the purple heads and was already talking to me again. But the name made my heart sink a little further. If it was going to be like this every time the phone rang and it wasn't Jen, my life was going to suck.

"Hi, Mandy."

"Hey, Hunter. Just wanted to catch up with you."

"Sure."

"First, let me say sorry for missing our meeting Friday."

I laughed, which hurt because of the cobblestone in my stomach. So those were the rules: no mentioning the Jammers or the shoes. Mandy's lost weekend would be our little unspoken secret.

"That's okay, Mandy. I know it wasn't your fault. I'm just glad you're okay."

"Never better. Actually, I'm up for a promotion."

I nodded, feeling a little twinge of pain that Jen had called that one.

"But thanks for your concern. Greg told me you called. So did Cassandra. In fact, *everyone* told me about how worried you were. I may have seemed annoyed the last time I saw you, but I won't forget that you came looking for me."

"No problem, Mandy. Looking for you led to some . . . interesting adventures." The cobblestone rumbled at the words.

"So I hear. That's the other thing I wanted to call you about." She paused.

"What's up?"

"Well, there are issues around this weekend, things we need to let chill for a while. The client doesn't want to get connected with events at a certain launch party. Certain influential persons are annoyed, and we have constituency relations to consider."

"Oh." My mind translated slowly, however straightforward the text: The client didn't want the purple-headed powers-that-be to know about their deal with the Jammers. Those powers were very pissed off and would be for a while. "What does that mean, Mandy?"

"It means that I can't give you any work. Not for a while, anyway."

"Ah."

I saw it all clearly now: I was the fall guy. The only person that the *hoi aristoi* could get their purple hands on, the only thread that might lead to the Jammers. The client would be keeping its distance.

Everyone would.

"I'm really sorry about this, Hunter. I always liked working with you."

"Me too, with you. Don't worry about it."

"And you know, these things don't last forever."

"I know, Mandy. Nothing does."

"That's the spirit."

Five minutes later I was searching my shelves for more things to sell, and the phone rang again. Again I averted my eyes from the caller ID.

It's not her, it's not her. . . . Maybe ten times would do the trick. It was her.

"Uh," I said. (Which is like "yeah" but much, much less hopeful.)

"Meet me at the park. Where we first met. Thirty minutes okay?"

"Okay."

THIRTY-FIVE

"CAN I TAKE A PICTURE OF YOUR SHOE?"

She lowered the binoculars, turned to me, and smiled.

"I'll have you know these are patented."

I looked down: she'd redone her laces. They were a deep green now, threaded into a hexagon around the tongue, then knotting up in the middle, bringing to mind a cat's eye but sideways. Everything else was standard Logo Exile except for her jacket—sleek, black, and sleeveless, shining in the sun, oversized.

"Don't worry. My interest isn't professional," I said.

"Yeah, Mandy called and told me." She looked down. "Turns out I did get you fired after all. Just took a little longer than we thought."

"I'll live."

"I'm sorry, Hunter."

So that was why she'd called. She felt guilty. This was a mercy meeting.

My lips parted, but nothing came out. I wanted to tell her what I'd realized about the Jammers, but everything I needed to say was too big to fit in my mouth. Jen waited for a moment, then raised the binoculars to her eyes again.

"What're you looking at?" I managed.

"The Brooklyn waterfront."

I turned to stare across the river, where a few features of the navy yard were discernible in the expanse of industrial buildings, winding highways, and crumbling dock space.

Of course. Jen never gave up.

"'See you at the factory'?" I quoted. That's what Mwadi Wickersham had said after the *hoi aristoi* had broken in, all violet and violent. The Jammers had been scheduled to relocate on Monday, but with serious forces in motion against them, why not a day early?

"You figure they'll stay in Brooklyn?"

"Yeah. I think they belong in Dumbo."

"It's the cool part of town, I hear." We stood shoulder to shoulder. "Seen anything interesting?" I asked her.

"You weren't followed, were you?"

"Don't think so. Walked up through Stuyvesant Town, then back down along the river. Not much cover in Stuy Town."

"Good thinking."

"Roger that."

She smiled, said, "Roger this," and handed me the binoculars.

They were heavy, military, camo-printed. Our fingertips touched for a moment.

The waterfront jumped into detail before my eyes, every quiver of my hands amplified into an earthquake. I steadied my grip, following a bicyclist along the Brooklyn Promenade.

"What am I looking for?"

"Check out the Domino Sugar factory."

I swept ahead of the bicycle, everything a blur with my speed. Then the familiar, long-stained factory walls flashed across my view. I backtracked, found the unlit neon letters of the name, the diagonal sugar chute that connected two buildings. Finally, a small, empty lot between the factory and the river.

"Rental trucks," I said softly. A few figures moved between the trucks and an open loading dock. "Jen, did you ever trace the license number of the truck we saw in front of the abandoned building?"

"Uh, no. Turns out I have no idea how to do that."

"Me neither. But . . . have you ever seen professional movers wearing all black? In summer?"

"Never. And see how they're parked? All squeezed up against the wall like that, so you can't see them from the street."

I lowered the binoculars. The trucks were grains of yellow rice to the naked eye, the human figures no bigger than iron filings moved by a hidden magnet. "They weren't expecting anyone to be watching them from Manhattan."

"Yeah, those field glasses were fourteen hundred bucks. Former Soviet Union military. But the guy said I can return them tomorrow if I don't like them."

"Jesus, Jen." I handed the binoculars back very carefully.

She raised them to her eyes, leaned against the railing, the binoculars' neck strap dangling over the water now. "The client must have coughed up some serious cash for the shoes. I heard they were turning those buildings into residential condos. Beautiful Manhattan views at a million a pop."

"Not all of them, apparently. My guess is that they've got a TV studio in their part of the factory, an editing suite at least, and who knows what else. So the Jammers are probably zoned light industrial."

She smiled. "Postindustrial, you mean."

"Postapocalyptic."

"Not yet. But give them time."

We stood there in silence for a while, Jen following the movements across the river carefully, me just glad to be there—analyzing how the Brooklyn waterfront had changed over the years, watching Jen's buzzed hair ruffle in the wind, liking the way it felt to be beside her, even if this was as close as we'd get from now on.

"How do you like your jacket?" she said.

"My what?" Then a strobe of recognition flickered in my brain. I reached out, touching the black, silken surface with its pattern of tiny fleur-de-lis. It was the lining of my thousand-dollar disaster, now on the outside. The horrendous rip was gone, along with the sleeves, the seams re-sewn to pull the jacket's elegant lines into its new inside-out configuration.

"Whoa."

"Try it on." She slipped out of it.

It fit me as beautifully as it had two nights ago. Slightly better, as things sometimes do when they're inside out. And this new jacket—unexpectedly sleeveless, silken ersatz Japanese, and bow-tie resistant—didn't belong to the non-Hunter; it was all me. "Gorgeous."

"Glad you like it. Took all night."

Her hands felt the seams down the sides, ran across the breast pocket (originally inside, now out), felt the fit across the shoulders. Then they slipped around my waist.

"I'm sorry, Hunter."

I breathed out slowly, looking into her green eyes. Relief flooded through me, as if some terrible test were over. "Me too."

She looked away. "You weren't the one being a bitch."

"You were just telling the truth. Possibly in a bitchy way, but the truth. I watch too much. Think too much."

"It's what you do. And you do it in a really cool way. I like the stuff in your brain."

"Yeah, Jen, but you want to change things—and not just how people tie their shoes."

"So do you." She turned to look out across the river. "You were just trying to make me feel better yesterday, pretending the Jammers weren't such a big deal. Weren't you?"

"Not exactly." I took a deep breath, because in between crippling bouts of feeling sorry for myself all night, I'd actually thought about this. "Jen, I'm not sure about the Jammers. I think they shoot for easy targets. And they take risks with other people's brains. You can't just go around rewiring people without asking. The moment someone gets seriously hurt, the whole trickster thing kind of loses its quirky appeal, you know?"

She thought about this for a moment, then shrugged. "Maybe. But that just means they need us to help them out. Your analytical skills, your vast database of useless facts. And my, uh, original thinking or whatever. We can help them. And they're just so cool."

"I know they are." I remembered my first day at school here in New York, realizing how far down the pyramid I'd fallen. I was suddenly a dork; anyone could see from the moment I walked into class. And I could see in turn who the cool kids were. It was like they were glowing, bright razors, so sharp that it hurt to look at them. I've been able to spot the cool kids ever since, no matter how young or old they are.

But since that day, I've never really trusted them.

So why did I trust Jen? I wondered. This was the girl who'd broken up with me only twelve hours before over . . . a pile of shoes. Or rather hated me because I hadn't stayed there to help, oblivious to her conviction that if she lost this one chance with the Jammers, she'd lose her cool again, as easy as tripping over a crack in the sidewalk.

Which was a nutty thing to believe but very Jen.

Anyway, she'd stopped hating me now.

"Maybe we'd make them even cooler, Hunter."

I looked at her and laughed, knowing that I'd help her find them. Because Jen thought she needed them, and I needed her. "Sure, we would."

She looked at the factory. Shrugged. "I've got a present for you."

"Another one?" I said.

"The jacket wasn't a present. It was yours, bought and paid for."

I twinged. "Not paid for yet, actually."

She smiled and put the binoculars into her backpack (in their thick, padded, Soviet-era case, I was glad to see). Pulled out a paper bag. Before she even had it open, I caught a whiff of burned plastic.

"I told you I'd find one. You should have stayed with me. If I'd had some help, it might not have taken two whole hours." She unwrapped it carefully as she spoke. "Just one, right at the bottom of the pile."

My mouth dropped open.

The shoe had remained miraculously untouched by the heat, the panels still pliable, their silvery, liquid-metal shine unblemished. The laces ran through my fingers like tendrils of sand. The eyelets glittered, tiny bicycle spokes spinning in the sunlight.

I'd almost forgotten how good they were.

"Smells like the fire," Jen said. "But I stuck a couple of shoe deodorizers in it, and it's already better. Just give it time."

"I don't care what it smells like."

I needed this too, I realized. It didn't take much to rewire Jen. Her brain was something unique, poised to turn ten years old again at the drop of a paka-paka attack, ready for every rooftop emergency door or plummeting air shaft or secret revolution. But I hadn't felt this way in so long—like I could fly or at least dunk from the free-throw line, like the mortar in my brain was loosening. I took the shoe from her and held on tightly.

"Still think the Jammers are so bad?" Jen asked.

I swallowed, looked out over the river at the enemies of all I held dear, and gave them the Nod.

"They have their moments."

THIRTY-SIX

I OWNED THE SHOE FOR ABOUT THREE WEEKS. THEN MY CREDIT-CARD bill arrived. Drastic action was required.

"You can always buy a pair when they come out," Jen assured me.

"Yeah, but not with the real logo." I'd miss that bar sinister. As a certain French philosopher once said, "Man is the animal that says no."

But I couldn't say no to a certain credit-card company whose name is a four-letter word. So we called up Antoine to make sure he was working that day, said we had something important to show him, and went uptown.

Dr. Jay's, like hip-hop culture itself, appeared in the Bronx in 1975. They're still there and now all over town, selling shoes and tracksuits and all manner of sports gear made from synthetic materials with names like Supplex and Ultrah, space-age words to conjure images of robot courtesans.

"My man, Hunter," Antoine said, then gave Jen the Nod, which probably meant that he remembered what she'd said at the focus group and thought it had been pretty cool.

He led us to the back, through the good-natured chaos egged on by the store's awesome sound system: little kids running the carpet to test fit and feel, guys trying on jerseys to find that perfect length between waist and knee, reflective rainbows of team logos spinning on their racks.

We reached the sanctuary of the storeroom and squeezed ourselves between high shelves of boxes ranked by size and make, Antoine pushing a rolling library ladder out of our way.

"What's that smell?" he asked as the shoe box opened.

"Jet engine," Jen said matter-of-factly, unwrapping the shoe from its paper.

When it came into the light, Antoine's eyes began to shine. He took it gingerly from her hands, rotated it to every side in turn, checking eyelets, tongue, laces, tread.

A minute later he whispered, "Where did it come from?"

"Bootleg," Jen said. "But they were all destroyed. That's the last one as far as we know."

"Damn."

"The client will be doing a version," I said. "But this is the original."

He nodded slowly, his eyes never leaving the shoe. "They won't do it right. Not like this. Some committee will mess it up."

"And it'll never have that." I pointed to the anti-logo.

He laughed. "Guess I won't be wearing them to work."

"There's no them. Only one survived."

"Damn."

I swallowed. "The thing is, I have to sell it. Serious money problems."

He looked at me, waiting for the catch.

"I *have* to sell it, okay?" I said.

"Huh. Never figured you like that, Hunter. But if you need the money, you need it."

"I do," I said, sounding like the groom at a shotgun wedding.

"How much?"

"Well, you see, I've got this credit-card bill, and it's about a thousand dollars—"

"Done."

It wasn't until we were out on the street, cash in hand, that I realized I could have asked for more.

The punch line to this tragic little tale is that the client never released the shoe. They never intended to.

Instead, they pirate little bits of it every season. Like Frankenstein's monster in reverse, the shoe is being slowly disassembled, its beautiful organs transplanted into a dozen different bodies.

You've probably seen the shoe yourself if you've kept your eyes on the ground, but only in pieces. It's easy to recognize, on the client's products and a dozen knockoffs and bootlegs—that part of any shoe that rewires your brain, makes you think for a moment that you can fly. But you'll never hold the whole thing in your hand. It went up in smoke.

Still, you can't blame the client for following the first rule of consumerism: Never give us what we really want. Cut the dream into pieces and scatter them like ashes. Dole out the empty promises. Package our aspirations and sell them to us, cheaply made enough to fall apart.

At least Antoine got good value for his money: he got the real thing.

And I got Jen.

We wound up kissing after the shoe was sold and gone, out on the street in the Bronx, me a little bit nervous about the thousand dollars stuffed into our pockets, big wads of small bills. (Try it sometime—it's pretty intense.) And after that we went back downtown and back to work, me knowing that I was following a compass whose needle swung toward trouble. Jen's an impact player, a spoiled brat, a royal pain in the ass, and she rewires me like nothing else. But things get better when she turns them inside out.

Which she usually does.

WHATEVER
CHAPTER

SO JEN AND I ARE STILL WATCHING THE JAMMERS, WAITING for their next move. But don't try this at home. They're cashed up, dressed to move, and if they catch you messing with them, they will turn your head purple.

Don't worry, though. You won't be left out. They're coming soon to a shopping mall near you. They have an agenda, and it includes everyone.

The Jammers are all around you, even if you can't see them. Well, okay, they're not exactly invisible. A lot of them have hair dyed in five colors, or wear six-inch platform sneakers, or carry enough metal in their skin that it's a hassle getting on an airplane. Pretty easy to spot, come to think of it.

But they don't wear signs saying what they are. After all, if you knew what they were up to, they couldn't work their magic. They have to observe carefully and delude and confuse you in ways you don't realize. Like good tricksters, they let you think you've discovered chaos on your own.

So you ask the question: What can the Jammers do, anyway? Won't they just fizzle like any other fad, fail like a million other revolutions, wind up useless and bitter, like an orphaned pile of pet rocks in the closet? Or can a small group of well-organized and charismatic Innovators really change the world?

Maybe they can.

By my reading of history, that's the way it's happened every time.

INNOVATORS HALL OF FAME

First person to jump out of an aircraft (a balloon) with a parachute:
André-Jacques Garnerin (1797)

First person to roll on classic "two-by-two" rollerskates:
James Plimpton (1863)

First person to reverse initial letters of two words to amusing effect:
Rev. William Archibald Spooner (1885)

First person to put ice cream in a cone:
Agnes B. Marshall (1888)

First person to go over Niagara Falls in a barrel:
Annie Edson Taylor (1901)*

*First person to tie shoelaces in the "double-helix" pattern:***
Montgomery K. Fisher (1903)

First company to produce canvas-top sneakers:
Keds (1917)

First person to cut clothing "on the bias":
Madame Madeleine Vionnet (1927)

---

* Don't try this at home. Or at Niagara Falls either.
** Also known as "the usual way."

First crowd to do "the wave":
Mexico City Olympics (1968)

First person to make a cell phone call from a NYC street:
Martin Cooper (1973)

First person to scratch a record on purpose:
Grand Wizard Theodore (1974-5)

First person to use the phrase "Future Sarcastic":
Cory Doctorow (2003)

The text of this book was set in 12.5-point Garamond. Based on the typeface created by sixteenth-century Parisian type designer Claude Garamond, this version was redesigned by Tony Stan in 1976.

The chapter titles in this book were set in Futura. Created in Germany in 1928, Futura is widely regarded as one of the most influential of the sans serif style of type faces.